The Book
of
Extremities

Other publications by Michael Glover:

Poetry:

Measured Lives (1994)
Impossible Horizons (1995)
A Small Modicum of Folly (1997)
The Bead-Eyed Man (1999)
Amidst All This Debris (2001)
For the Sheer Hell of Living (2009)
Only So Much (2011)
Hypothetical May Morning (2018)
Messages to Federico (2018)

Other:

The Trapper (2008)
Headlong into Pennilessness (2011)
Great Works: Encounters with Art (2016)
Playing Out in the Wireless Days (2017)
111 Places in Sheffield You Should Not Miss (2017)
Late Days (2018)
Neo Rauch (2019)
Thrust: the story of the cod-piece in art (2019)

As editor or contributor:

Memories of Duveen Brothers (1976)
Goin' down, down, down: Matthew Ronay (2006)
Robert Therrien (2016)
Monique Frydman (2017)

The Book
of
Extremities

Michael Glover

www.1889books.co.uk

For Lucy and Spencer

et La Commune de Géay

The Book of Extremities

Paroles domestiques —

Les bas sont sur le piano — —

en plein air plein

Poésie —

Le motif — com Ronsard, Mallarmé —
Difficulté de le développer —
Rares sont les pièces où il se prolonge) jusque ad

— La charpente — ou clavier
Corneille, Racine, La F — Virgile
Corneille le meilleur constructeur — — Hu
La F — le musicien —

— La phrase — Racine Retenu
Les retardements — !

distinction et rapports du discours parfait et du
le récitatif —

En français les "beaux vers" sont presque tous latins
les "beaux motifs" sont celtes (?) —
Le beau motif tient plus à la spontanéité, au parler
qui échappe tout formé.

L'Homme de Verre

Ma solitude – qui n'est que le manque depuis beaucoup d'années, d'*amis* longuement, profondément vus; de conversations étroites, dialogues sans préambules, sans finesses que les plus rares, elle me coûte cher. Ce n'est pas vivre que vivre sans objections, sans cette résistance vivante, cette proie, cette autre personne, adversaire, reste individué du monde, obstacle et ombre du moi – autre moi – intelligence rivale, irrépressible – ennemi le meilleur ami, hostilité divine, fatale, intime...

extrait du *Log-Book de Monsieur Teste*, Paul Valéry

A Note on the Text by a Friend

From time to time the author of this fragmentary work has quoted, often quite randomly, and as the mood has happened to seize him (or so it seems to me, and I must point out from the start that I myself am not an intellectual man), from the words of the French poet Paul Valéry, of whose writings he was so inordinately fond. In fact, they were always on his lips. More so than his own words, it has to be said, because my friend said very little when not required to do so.

My greatest sadness is that my friend never knew Valéry, in spite of the fact that their lives overlapped – by which I mean that they were briefly alive at the same time. Perhaps this is all to the good. I believe – and I have thought of this so often, and especially since his death – that he did not really want to meet him. He could have written to him in the guise of a young admirer or disciple. I would urge him to do so from time to time. Those letters were never written. He would tell me that he was never in a state of sufficient preparedness. I am not convinced.

This may sound a little harsh on my friend, but I think that he never wanted to have any contact with him. It was better that way. He could talk to him more easily, and perhaps – who knows? – even uninterruptedly, because he knew that his famous interlocutor would always be absent. The Valéry that he knew so well was the Valéry that he himself had invented, and that is exactly as it should be. Valéry himself would have been too exalted and intimidating a personage to deal with. His presence would have spoiled the dream. It would, furthermore, have got in the way of what I conjecture to be some of my old friend's more fanciful surmises and appropriations. That said, I love him still, and I would not have devoted several years of my life preparing this text for publication if I did not think that it was a work of great literary merit. My friend did not instruct me to do so. By no means. Nor did he specifically ask me to destroy it, so my conscience is clear. He gave it to me during the last months of his life, soon after he had lost his sight, with nothing but a characteristically dismissive nod of the head.

The text itself was interrupted by death, and I have it organised as well as I have been able - he left nothing but a collection of fragments, each one written on a separate piece of paper.

HONNEUR A LA MEMOIRE DES ENFANTS DE LA COMMUNE DE GEAY MORTS POUR LA FRANCE

AMIOT Edgard

BREAUDEAU George

BREDEAU Léonce Caporal

BOUTIN Jean

BOUTIN Paul

CAILLAUD Albert

CHABOT Louis

CHARPENTIER Clément

DANIER Paul

GACHET Léonce

GARLOPEAU Ernest

GILBERT Henri

GRELAUD Aristide

JOULIN Léon

LATOUR (de) Jehan Colonel

LATOUR (de) Olivier Capitaine

LATOUR (de) Hubert s/Lieutenant

MAISSANT Maurice

MARTIN René

MOINE Louis

NOUREAU Léopold

PARFAIT Louis

QUERE Edmond

ROUSSEAU Alexandre

RICHAUDEAU Francois

1939-45

CHANCELLE René

ROBION Henri

GUERRE D'INDOCHINE

George, Lolas, sergent

May I soon join them, Lord. As you so wish.

I hate writing. To write disgusts me. I cannot tell a story. I cannot listen to a story. I have nothing but contempt for storytellers, those pedlars of dreams. To tell a story is to lie, and I would not wish to lie. All that I have, and all that I wish to vouchsafe of the truth of myself, is here. I give you myself, in all my foolishness, all my culpability, all my errancy. I have made many choices in my life, many mistaken choices.

*

And there is something else too. I speak here only of moments, the spasmodically seized, the discontinuous. This is my truth as far as I can tell it. It is all that I know. You see, I cannot stray far. I do not have the mental capacity to stray far.

*

There you have me then, in all my acknowledged limitations. If you are already inclined to toss me aside in exasperation, then do so now. There are many other more enriching diversions. On the other hand, when weighed in the balance, all this, being brief and therefore relatively inconsequential, may seem worthy of your attention...

*

Do not expect me to change. Do not expect more than this mere smattering of words.

I

Le Lavoir. That most ancient of places. The dank green of the pool, unmoving. Another day to see and be seen there. By whom? Those bygone ghosts? How I arrived there today, I do not exactly know. And, a little later, a radical shift in the angle of the light at the top right-hand corner of the kitchen window.

I am killing no one but myself.

II

No, not Schubert's *Death and the Maiden*, not this morning. Something spikily achromatic in its stead, in keeping with the fissures in the walls of this house – above the *cheminée*, for example – where I have plied my trade of snatching souls – since time immemorial or so it seems – from certain death by drowning. I speak metaphorically, of course.

III

The lowest order of windows, as seen from this room, the sweep of it around the exaggeratedly long apsidal end, is in fact a series of blind arcades, each one closed off by a patchwork of soft, honey-coloured stone. Consequently, the interior of the church is very dark. I feel my way forward there, every day. It is forty years now. Can that really be so? It really is so.

IV

I cannot think not to pray because it is always there outside the window, when I rise in that hour before dawn, and when I go to bed, the church, in all its massiness, its ancientness, its dignified,

accusatory indomitability. It will never not watch over me. Is this what I always wanted for myself? Yes, I find myself saying.

V

The ivy clings like a lizard to the boundary wall of the garden of this house, and I begin to rip at it with my bare hands. Meanwhile, the bees are humming in the sprawling lavender bushes at my back. God be praised for all fruitful things, the predators and the preyed upon. He has made them all.

VI

Coolness and heat. Heat and coolness. The temperature changes from moment to moment. The sky is wiped clean of its clouds, like the blackboard in the *Ecole Maternelle* beyond the *Mairie*, that detestable place, where the man sits, both palms wiped clean. Did they not once shine with the oozing grease of his unhallowed sweat?

VII

I was not born here. And yet I must die here. I have my allotted place in the graveyard. I stare at it, daily. I tend to it. If no one was at my back to observe me, I would surely kneel.

VIII

I pinch the lavender between thumb and finger. I inhale its sweet, narcotising aroma. Meanwhile, the bees encircle me angrily. Or perhaps they merely simulate anger. Who can know – I mean truly know – the mood of the bee, for all its excitability?

IX

I build this text, word by word, as if it were the stones of a house; in fact, as if it were the very house in which I live, here, for the years remaining to me: *La Maison du Curé, 6 Allée du Prieuré, Géay.*

X

Language, language itself, is so destructive. I wish that I could stop and start again. I build it so badly. I am such a clumsy, ham-fisted workman.

XI

None of this, you must understand, is for publication, Paul, my dear Paul. You know that. You have my specific instructions to destroy all these words of mine. Do not betray me. You have promised not to betray me.

XII

The wind has climbed as high as my head, and now it has wrenched off my hat, and sent it spinning across the churchyard. I walk after it, pleading for it to stay still, please. I move forward, with a measure of dignity.

XIII

I have secured the shutters back by their metal clasps. The banging of shutters in the dead of night is the worst of all evils. It feels like a presentiment of sorts.

XIV

I write all this down between four and seven in the morning, when
all is clear and unsullied – the air at this hour is singing – and the
mind battens down upon its objectives, straight, swift, sure as any
arrow.

XV

This afternoon the side door of the house was thrown back like a
ravening maw. I jumped up from my chair and quickly closed it.

XVI

Entirely for myself and no one else. There is no one else. I am at
last free to speak the truth, albeit whisperingly.

XVII

This house is my representative. It is my breath, my lungs, my
heart. It can never disappear from me. It can never unbuild itself.
What passing wind just then called me a liar?

XVIII

There is always this terrible openness, an openness to the sky
perhaps. What if things are not at all as they seem to be?

XIX

These blind arcades are my multiple emptinesses, my obstructions,
my saying no, no, no to myself.

XX

When the clouds rise, I rise up with the clouds. When the clouds
fall, I fall with the clouds. They take on my shape. I take on their
ever shifting shapes.

XXI

The lavender bushes have taken two steps backwards. At that
point, I make my apologies and disappear into the house.

XXII

Marie has gone through the house today, and laid one thing upon
another as if everything deserves everything else, as if there are
rhythms to be imposed.

XXIII

A blight. An inconsolableness. Where, if not here? Whither, if not
there? Is it my good neighbour's tomato crop that I am addressing?

XXIV

Two structures are in their proper contexts: that church and this
house.

XXV

We shrink as the spaces narrow.

XXVI

This house is four-square, of the Enlightenment. Its pediment is Hellenic and entirely reasonable. The church, though cruciform, smacks of unruliness due to an unruly spillage of people. Why did I once say that to myself?

XXVII

The nodding violence of the hollyhocks disturbs my peace of mind.

XXVIII

What does any man, no matter how fine and upstanding, really know of himself?

XXIX

Do not forget. There is a pitiful bleating for unity here, a thirsting for coherence, amidst all this fragmentation. Let the truth be spoken. It must toll like a bell.

XXX

To grow up such and such a one. To be buffeted, pinched, mocked, scalded by insults, and still to remain standing upright in the schoolyard. And then to walk away.

XXXI

I said to myself just then: let me emerge from all this feebleness, this frailty. No longer to fear the spider or the next oncoming storm!

XXXII

He who can. He who cannot. He who must. He who must not.

XXXIII

I have reached a certain level of emotional desiccation. No one has demanded this of me. I have chosen to be as I have been. Spare me the worst of it, Marie.

XXXIV

I run my hands across the plain boards of this table. I love its fidelity, its unbending affection, its willingness to support my books.

XXXV

Why would you wish, now, to say so much when you have said so little for so long?

XXXVI

The noise – the threat – of industry: bees in the lavender bushes.

XXXVII

The metal rods at the top of the flight of steps which leads up to the side door of this house are either rusting or absent. It would be possible – at any hour of the day or night – to jump and break a leg.

XXXVIII

Cobbled. Edged with lengths of stone. A niche at its end. One stone seat for the women, who were obliged to take it in turns, day by day. A high wall surrounding. Fed by the waters of the *rivière*. Water a sultry, cloudy green today. Pocked by rain. Long since unused. Entranceway, with its great stone lintel. Could it be here? Could it have been here? I find myself saying.

XXXIX

Extreme physical fragility has never been a problem for me. I throw all my strength into the dissection of the spirit.

XL

First she would turn my face to the wall of the *cave*, pressing my forehead into its rough irregularities, and then she would begin to scratch at my scalp with her long, cracked finger nails, quite slowly at first, as if to soothe me. She would sing to me, thinly, waveringly, tunelessly. I would listen, rapt. And yet I was not soothed. I was already conjuring worlds of my own devising. I was already losing myself within myself.

XLI

Let me pace this room out, from wall to windows, from wall to door, from *cheminée* to deep-set hearth with its wood-burning stove, my *Jotul*. Now let all this grow inside me until it becomes an enormous space, particular to myself alone, in which to breathe and to flourish.

XLII

Let me confide this to you now. It has never ceased growing. That is why there is no reason to leave this place, because it has become my everywhere. I could not wish for more. I am truly blessed, am I not?

XLIII

The bell at noontide – how its notes bend and waver in the air! – brings back the labourers from the fields, gnawing at their knuckles.

XLIV

With that extreme physical fragility comes a tremendous alertness to danger, danger, danger.

XLV

I write all this to separate myself from myself. Do I also write all this to separate myself from you, whoever you may be? When you arrived today, I separated myself from myself in order to avoid you. I walked through the door. I flew out of the window, quite effortlessly. I waved at you. You continued to talk to me. Nothing of you has changed. Nothing of you will ever change.

XLVI

Everything, in this deafening hive of uncertainties.

XLVII

The strength of this space – these plastered walls, these roof beams
– supports my weakness, raises me up to be likewise, strong and
four-square. To be engulfed by fantasies.

XLVIII

Without careful systematisation, all must surely be lost. To group.
To reconcile. To render peaceably juxtaposed.

XLIX

I do not like myself. I do not love myself. If I were to nourish or
encourage certain feelings of tenderness, would I applaud myself
for having done so? No, surely not. The best must be a measure of
indifference. And therein exists a certain equilibrium, a soothing
stasis of sorts.

L

I cannot read a book from beginning to end. It is altogether too
wearisome. Words, individual words, snag on me. I pull one out
and examine it in the round. I hold it up to the light, wonderingly.
It teases me. It leads me away. I simply cannot proceed rapidly,
sentence by successive sentence. I have this compulsion to dig
deep, and ever deeper, into less and less. How far – how near – is
the extent of myself?

LI

What is more, I have so little. My gestures are few, my words
spasmodic. I feel so little. There is so little of me to give away, to
pass from hand to hand, to offer to someone else. This is why I

have called on God to replenish me with the tiniest droplet from his superabundance.

LII

There is no space in my life for sentiment.

LIII

Her ugliness is boundless. I see her proceeding across the churchyard, mop and bucket in hand, clod-hopping. She barely speaks.

LIV

Several hundred fragments. Mosaics in a wall. How do they bond?

LV

To chart the movement of the waters. Are they unstirring today?

LVI

The fine filaments of the cobwebs. To carry them, unwillingly, between the knuckles or in the hair. To disperse the spiders, entire families, at the open window, blowing them, lightly, into the air. I love these spiders. I love them when they are elsewhere. I could say the same of myself. I could say the same of you.

LVII

How the body is carried this morning, how it seems to be *carrying itself,* so lightsomely, as if in a false mood of gaiety, nudged forward by the slightest of slight breezes, and, at my back, nothing at all...Unless I am mistaken, of course. Unless there is a shadow again – that call, that distant call, of her shadow...

LVIII

I sit here, burying myself ever more deeply into this chair at my upstairs window as I gaze. At dawn there are these clottings of mist between the trees where the valley begins to fall away. They trap the trees in a froth, a welling foam, of sorts. Their summits are offered up to me – all the rest has been snatched away – as if to say: take, eat... And then they are gone. Just as I go to reach out, they are snatched from me. That is the way of things hereabouts. And I am resigned to it all. It is in my nature to be so resigned.

LIX

The poet I call my friend has just now returned from his journeyings. He sits here exactly where I sit, bony elbows propped on the edge of this wooden table beside the window, amongst my books and my pens, staring down at his unruly words, his fine head wreathed in tobacco smoke. Yes, the heady odour of tobacco smoke. That is the milieu in which his thoughts swim. I watch him, attentively, through the haze. I see him, and I see into him. It is as if I am invested with certain magical powers of penetration. I see how the words turn and turn in his head, running, leaping, pirouetting, so balletically. I would emulate him if I could. If he were not my master, he would be my help-mate, my friend. *Paul.* I have said his name. Just the once. And to myself. God forbid that I should distract him from his labours.

LX

I ask myself what sort of thing this is. It is a deposit, a clump, a massy pile. I have no wish to tiptoe around it. Let it lie exactly where it is, stinking or not.

LXI

I call none of this mine. It is too distant from me. It does not answer me when I call. It does not speak back to me. It merely keeps its place, entirely properly, as if it has worlds of its own to care about. And so it must be. I cannot begrudge it its separateness from me. Nothing I do will enable me to engulf it. I am too small and too powerless.

LXII

I willed myself to be perfectly still. I lay like a board, arms rigid at my sides. I was a mere child then, playing at death, embracing the smoky haze of my own future. When she called up to me from the bottom of the ladder, I would hear the sound of my name being spoken. I would listen to its music. Its music would give me the most exquisite pleasure. I would not answer. I knew never to answer. I knew to strip her away from me, to lay her aside. I suffered the crime of self-abandonment. It was a pact that I entered into with myself, a holy pact. A most unholy pact.

LXIII

Is it too much to wait here with such patience? Am I expecting too much of myself? Is it true that he will never return, that I will never step out, that there will never be any kindly gesture of reciprocity? Yes, all these things are true. And it is for this reason that I embrace them so wholeheartedly. They are all a part of me. I am such a patchwork of selves. No wonder there is such giggling in the streets, such a gentle tittering behind cupped hands.

LXIV

There is always such a pacing of the boards of this floor. I listen to my regular tread. I take comfort from it. It is as pure and dependable as a steady heart beat. The problem is, I whisper to myself, that I am going nowhere. Every day I am going nowhere at this same steady pace, and it so pleases me. Every day I feel a little richer from my journeyings.

LXV

You have created nothing but this, I say to myself, staring down at the palm of my hand. And is this sufficient? I raise it. I let it fall. I weigh it in the air's fine balance. It is sufficient, it is insufficient, it is gnarled, it is wizened. It is so much smaller and delicate-fine than it used to be. Can I not almost see through it? Why then does it move from side to side, with such fury, when it grips the pen? What is gaining on it? Why such hurry?

LXVI

I am not alone with myself because there is always the possibility of conversation when I read my own words back to myself. I have staked out such and such a territory, and now I must fight to reclaim it. It is no easy business.

LXVII

I have asked Paul exactly what it is that he is after. There is such a dedication to the cause. Hour after hour he sits at this table – my old, familiar table – staring down at his words. I say to myself: one day he will rise to greet me. He will offer me his hand in fellowship. He will say to me: we two are like-minded. That is what I am waiting to hear, those words from his lips: we two. It will be such a solemn compact, as if between the living and the dead. His pen rises, darts, scurries from place to place – there is no such thing as an even, regular motion. And then it stops again, poised, mid-air, as if it must surely always know when to stop and when to start again, as if it knows where it is always destined to go. There is such gravity, such a dignity, in all of this, such deep-rooted assurance that the journey always has its purpose, its goal. And I stand by, reverentially silent, thinking to myself: I am nothing but a swept heap of fallen, shrivelled leaves, ever ready to be dispersed by the wind.

Her *balai* stands in the corner of the kitchen, waiting. That is its place.

LXVIII

When I return, even from the briefest of brief distances, it is as if I have never been away. I greet my wheelback chair again, at its familiar, awkward angle to the kitchen table. I place my hand across its back, feelingly. I grip it with a fierce amiability. And then I find myself pausing to wonder. It is as if a shadow has fallen across me. Can it really be true, I say to myself, that I have been away at all, even as far as the lane? Perhaps, in fact, I never stirred. Perhaps I merely imagined myself rising up from the chair, inching my way down the four stone steps to the garden, greeting the lavender bushes in passing, and then, having carefully swung closed

the gate, slowly proceeding down the lane, listening to my feet crunch down upon the gravel. Perhaps all that never happened. Perhaps I was merely sitting here all this time, in my chair at the table, staring down into the sludgy dregs of this bowl of coffee, watching myself writing the words which were conjuring such a scene, the very ones that you are currently reading.

LXIX

So much is fury and confusion, day after punishing day. I know it for certain. I will never match up. I will never rise to the occasion. Why do I torture myself then in this way? Why do I say to myself: when you are finished, this may be the equal, what you are doing here, of the words of the master. It is all such a futile endeavour. You know that you cannot write.

LXX

And so you must begin again. To begin again is to be freshly alive, resurrected from the ashes of yourself. Where there was such hopelessness, there may yet be fresh hope. Call yourself a mewling, pestering, bawling, unruly child again if you like. A child blunders. A child knows nothing. A child sees as if through a mist of unknowing. Above all things else, a mere child lacks the burden of self-consciousness. No reasonable argument prevents him from hastening forward, pell mell, in the direction of a fulfilment, a freedom, as yet unglimpsed. He has an unbridled enthusiasm for life. It is this that you have lost. And it is this that you must re-find if you are not to be given up as a ghost. If you were to become as a child again, you would be re-born. You would not be disgusted by these words of yours. You would not erase them, in a fit of boiling exasperation, with such fierce strokes of the pen – as you just now did.

LXXI

Late afternoon. A general spirit of late-summer fatigue and decline, in and out. Randomly picking about in the shadow of the boundary wall that fronts the house. Picking about, bent over, in a supreme posture of indignity, simian-like. So small a space. Six square metres in all, I estimate. And yet it is sufficient. It is more than sufficient. Bending over in order to grab at and wrestle with tussocks of hardy weed that have forced their way through the gravel. With sweat-drenched brow, I rise up to the vertical again, holding them fast in my grip, admiring them so in all their perversity. The sheer, no-holds-barred tenacity of weeds. Their indomitability. Their refusal to take no for an answer. Their furious posturing. Must I forever be lacking the strength, the purpose, the wilfulness of a mere weed? I listen out for an answer. A single small stone stares back at me.

LXXII

There is no hopefulness in prayer, not any more. Prayer consists of words, mere words, randomly scattered in the teeth of the wind. Words in no particular order. Words of no particular moment. Words of no usefulness. Words of no gravity. Unilluminating words, massy and messy as clods. Why do I still use such things? Why are they upon my lips on waking? Why do I hear them bandied about in these parts as if, to some, they still give pleasure? I must disown them. Let me disown them. Yes, let me say such a thing as this without the meaningless burden of words coming between. To be felled by such a paradox.

LXXIII

The freshness of winter on these bare knuckles. They look tight, almost transparent. The sharp, harsh, unremitting bite of it.

Sniffing the cold of the air like a wary fox in a field. Frost is so near. It is on days such as these that my flesh creeps closer to me, like a long gone companion just now returning home. I hug myself to myself. I make a gift of myself to myself, huddled here as I am, in these old grey blankets, in front of my table at the window, looking out onto the dense, enfolding fog of my native habitat. All human kind has drawn back, self-protectively. I hear scarcely anything at all. I see barely any one – just one or two perhaps, every other day, almost running, and close to the ground, as if to escape back into their lives of the utmost privacy. It was on such a day as this, I tell myself, that God himself was born, springing his great surprise upon the world.

LXXIV

I cradle a warm singing in my ears this morning. I am lit up by it. I do not feel my body as I rise up from the bed, weightless as a feather. Who is guiding me down these stairs? Who stands beside the sink, lovingly preparing my cup of coffee? And then, just as quickly, Paul is gone, leaving the door ajar, with all life's chill winds blowing at me. I hurry over. I peer. I am still peering.

LXXV

There is no sweeter or straighter path than this one, bordered with such flowers, I am saying to myself as I walk, bent of head, through the oncoming rain. My eyes rise to take in the wicker casket, the spill of white roses, and the lilies, with their trumpets, which neither wove nor spun. They are holding it up for me, the six, united in due solemnity. I go to touch it. She rests in the ground, saying nothing, and then slowly she rises above the houses, pointing the way. My eye easily follows the arrowing of her finger. I blink awake. Today I cannot feel my own hands. I try to find her again. I see nothing.

LXXVI

Who are you to ask me to account for it all?

LXXVII

How and where it happened. It is all a haze and then, of a sudden, I see it again, as if I am freshly jolted awake by the school bell. A lightning strike? Nothing more nor less. In my bed. And then: the sudden eruption of a theatrical performance. They are carrying me above their heads, down the stairs, and I am not protesting. Not even so much as a mouse's squeak beneath the boards of this floor. In fact: this is inevitable, I am saying to myself, let it now speed towards its inevitable conclusion. Part of the wall had fallen away – the chimney breast, in the kitchen. There was nothing but a hollowed space of such and such a size, so perfectly calculated. And I, stiff as a board, am being raised up so that I can be measured against it. They all nod, in unison, turning me, raising me, to a just height, inserting hooks into my shoulder blades so that I can be hung there, perfectly anchored and poised, facing into the room from that alcove, as an enduring testament to my own life. And then there begins the slow, sure work of plastering over, slopping it into the gaping, wondering, gagging mouth until I almost choke, smearing it over the tremulous bulging of the eye balls. And I, I am prepared for all of this. I accept that soon enough I will see nothing, that I will be saying to myself forever after: you have the full consolation of the deposits of memory. Remain vigilant for just as long as you are able. And so I have remained.

LXXVIII

They will always be dead. That is why the memorial in their memory has been raised up so close to the church, so that I can look from one to the other, from the names of the dead to the great, coffined space behind them. For that is what it is: an almighty, near lightless coffin. I see it all now. It has never been clearer to me. When I kneel in reverence, I entomb myself. Was it better to die in those fields than here? That is the question I must forever be asking myself.

LXXIX

I know you by your name and by the looks you occasionally give me, side-on, sheepish. Very few of them. I tiptoe awkwardly around you. I thank you, curtly, graciously. I apologise to you for my habits of absent-mindedness, for the careless strewing of books across surfaces. I thank you for the soup, on a Friday, and for the vegetables too, washed clean of soil. There is little more to be said. You strip my bed. You wash my clothes, my vestments. You will doubtless wash my cerements too, given your youthfulness. I am grateful to you. I mouth these words of thanks as I watch you, from this window, retreating down the lane, heaving your sackful. You are a beast of burden, a blessed, near dumb beast, and I need you.

LXXX

This is a day like no other. It is His day. I look out for Him everywhere. Have the very trees shaped themselves in acknowledgment? The cold clenches. I grit my teeth as I walk, gripping the key. I try to prevent myself shivering. No one sees me. No one greets me. I stare down at my feet as I walk across the grasses, so crisply frosted. This is His day. I say it to myself once again, and then over and over, until its echoings shake me to the very foundations. And then, from nowhere, a pigeon rises, flinging itself up into the air like a house cloth being shaken of its dust from a window, and I smile. I smile. I smile.

LXXXI

One day she lost her arm, the arm which held the Sword of Faith. It was there. And then it was gone. One slow morning, winter gaining, when sunlight splashed the nave with its hosannas, I entered, and saw that it was so. I stood beneath her, wonderingly. No one had entered. No one had left again. And yet it was gone. Broken off. The Sword of Faith. I experienced then, through all the pain of loss, a new lightness, as if I had shrugged something off, an old, dull, heavy carapace of sorts.

LXXXII

Paul has said it to me again: there is no such thing as the savoursomeness of memory. Memories are always insubstantial, inaccurate blurrings. You must not pretend to live by them. They tell you no truth. They merely haunt you. These tiny, floating dust motes in the air – he pointed just then – are better by far. We know nothing of them, do we? he said, turning to face me. We merely wonder at them. We snatch at them in play, and they are not there. I looked. I nodded. I returned to my book. I recorded his every word, his every gesture.

LXXXIII

It is this fear of making anything. I am not a maker. Words! Words! Words! They tumble out of this lumpish sack of myself in no particular order. There is a cacophony of sounds when I say them over to myself in this room. The very walls bend and flap, as if in mockery. Harsh, grating, swollen excrescences. Let me insult my own words. Let me call them to order, dress them down, humiliate them in all their preposterousness. It is so much easier when I turn away to watch the world outside this window, when I am separated from the world by the silence of this window.

LXXXIV

Every day I watch them walking, unknowing, across the grasses, weaving between the tombs. I follow the light lifting of their legs, their quick steppings, the way the satchels beat down upon young backs as they run, those satchels, a-bulge with the beginnings of all earthly knowledge. Knowledge comes, only to go again. It does not stay with us. It is an unfaithful friend. We build a fine, towering edifice throughout the length of our days, and then we watch, with slow patience, as it begins to tumble back again into the dust, the dust of long forgotten ages. What was it exactly that I knew when I was said to know something? Could I have been said to know myself? What exactly is this I that I have, life-long, been pursuing? Does it bring me comfort? Does it even recognise me?

LXXXV

I dream of nothing quick and nothing wasteful. A slow, patient, particular scooping out of the earth from the mouth of the flower pot, to make a socket for this rose, which is already fading. Why would I plant a rose in a pot outside this window which is already fading? And then I am suddenly awake and the rose, of course, has blown.

LXXXVI

Seven of a winter morning, and I am here again, clasping myself to myself, beside my desk at this window, pent, expectant. Do I feel my feet, my hands? No matter. I try to remain perfectly still - as a tree, perhaps, is perfectly rooted when it is not buffeted by the storms of life. Here I am again then, in all my transparency, my frivolity, my foolishness, my thirsting after the coming dark. I peer out, but my eyes are strangely clouded. There are distant floatings and stirrings. A mouse scurries. My heart goes out to it, but it is a little too quick for me. I begin to close this notebook, but I do not want to be done with it. The interrogation will never end. I do not want it to end. As long as it is here, it is a register of my presence, and I would not fade so soon, so willingly. And yet I would, willingly. And so the pendulum swings in the air.

LXXXVII

Paul, do I try to emulate your sighs, your uneasy shiftings in that chair over there, where you sit facing the sea, that sea into which you plunge, as man and boy, with such fierce gaiety, even as you remain seated here with your back to me? I would be there too, hair sleek and streaming, beside you. Let me come to you. Now you are rising to leave, in such a hurry, straightening your collar, and you are shortly to be married, just beyond that sunlit door. The organ calls in due solemnity. Tears of joy spill for you. But nothing goes right. She is ailing again. She is calling, calling, and throwing out to you the pale, theatrical arm of her neediness, again and again. Which means that you cannot work. You close the door, and again you close the door, but she is always in front of you, lying prone in her daybed, between you and your desk. You cannot work. And for all that, you despise the frivolity of literature, and so you are not clear, not exactly, in what your work should consist. Ideas are your forte, but what are these ideas, and where will they lead you? O my confusion of sorrows, must you forever be thirsting, and is that why you need me to talk to you, *sotto voce*, just the two of us, in this way? Is this why we are so mutually sustaining? Tell me before you fade again. Turn to me with some brief words of reassurance.

LXXXVIII

Let me say it now lest others say it for me, and thereby cause resentment: there has been a great loss. A loss of nerve perhaps. A diminution, a quiet thinning out, of the will. A loss of the future. The future is quite blown away, as if it were no more substantial and dependable than a drift of afternoon cloud. No tree in this garden says: look at me. Nothing calls out to me. The grasses of the churchyard have no desire to be walked upon. Even the key to the church has gone missing. And so here I am now, with this room pivoting about me. I drift aimlessly, from wall to wall. I lift the sticks and arrange the paper in the fireplace. There is no particular order to be sought for in any arrangement of sticks and paper. And the flames, when they rise, rise in no particular order. There is no shapeliness to the flames on this fierce winter morning. I do not admire them for their shapeliness. I have no use for such a word.

LXXXIX

I have caused it all to happen. I have caused nothing to happen. I have stood by helplessly as my own life has shaped itself out of this strange and ungainly medley of limbs, tissues, organs, and all sluiced with my own life blood. I have played no part in it all. I have been the bland observer. I have never seized hold of myself and said to myself: this is what you are to be. I have been nothing, with perfect consistency. I have run after myself, calling. I have said to myself, pleadingly: please turn around so that I can stare you in the face, so that I can recognise you for who or what you are. But I have never listened to or heeded my call. I have continued to walk ahead of myself at an even pace, supremely indifferent to my own pesterings.

XC

The leaves are bantering. The stones are chattering. So much in this way. So much in the way of things. In flight past this window, such eager, headlong flight, and caught again. Eye goodness. I serve them all. I give of myself. I peel myself away, layer by layer. I chafe at my bones. And, little by little, I reduce myself to nothingness. Is that its way? But wait. They are also my helpmates. I console myself here, in this beloved space of all my days. It is quite as much as is needed. It is more than enough. One stone would be more than sufficient. He has added and added, from his great abundance. Thank you. And then thank you. Kneeling on the cold earth, tilting the head skyward with a new and fuller openness to the air. Gulping it down. He has given me stones without number, heaped and then strewn, ground to the finest of gravels. And the leaves are a covering for my nakedness. It was inevitable (or so they say) when all else falls away. My green dress, bright-shining, of new hope. How they cling to me, so seductively. Brotherly. Sisterly.

XCI

I have not walked past this window. I have not seen him walk past this window. I was only ever asleep in this chair. Not exactly asleep. Awake, though somnolent, drooped over in a smooth curve, catching the smudged light of a cloudy day. And forever attentive to the heart beats, slow, slow, and then a little quicker, if not skipping with excitability. Attentive to the quicksilver foragings of the mind, which travels who knows when or whither. Paul and I together, he in the lead, and I pulled after, as if driven on by a wind from behind, which knows where I must go. After and then after. He peered in then, and saw me. He denied my presence there. He said: the house is empty. As empty as an uninhabited sleeve. As empty as bygone days must surely be forever empty. I said to him: the chair and I are as one. I picked up the chair then. I brandished it in the air. I said: look, feel. How to deny such solidity, such weaponry. I brandished it, fiercely upthrusting. He said to me, laughter peeling away: it is a chair, leaping and dancing, it is a chair, and it is, by some miracle, self-sustaining. I sat on the chair again. I gave it the full force of my fury, and it sustained me, for I am as a reed in the wind, much to be pitied, though there are none hereabouts, at the keen top edge of this field, facing this church and its green acres of the dead, to pity me, and yet I have no regrets. Let me say that over until it rings in the air: I have no regrets.

XCII

Note this now. The fingers' quick flights, with pen at a certain angle to the vertical. From eye/mind to finger, threading down through the air. And all connections invisible. Acrobatics of sorts. High-wheeling outflingings, and all invisible. Every morning it was the same, pulling the threads together, interweaving them, like the spider's astonishing diagonals, through those arabesques of cigarette smoke, and as noiselessly busy as the spider. And such fine, spidery calligraphy. And, like the spider, no one to be attentive to the task, no one to regard it as of paramount importance, this unlocking and unloosing of all that he was, the lying out, year after patient year, during those dawn hours, of all that he was, the treasures of it all, his mystery. And no one to read, no one to convince or to be convinced, but he. And now: I.

XCIII

What do I see when I read them over, these words of mine? I see nothing fine or studied. And what do I hear when I say them over to myself? I merely hear the regular dull hammerings of the anvil, day after day. I am a slave to my task. And yet the task itself is not unworthy of me because I myself am of so little worth. The least little would surely be a triumph, much more than I ever deserved. The difficulty is this: how to have the temerity to share it. Who has pronounced it valuable? Who has looked over my shoulder and appraised my words, counted them fine and worthy? Has he? Has he? No, he has not judged me.

XCIV

I am alive now, strangely vivid to myself, at a certain leaning angle
to the boards of this floor, as if I were a building not yet fully
realised. There are other angles, other posturings, other more
violent forms of self-representation. The bean. The pumpkin. The
sunflower. Those are three such. I suck myself in and I expand
myself, willingly. All is premeditated. I could crawl. I could howl. I
could powder my hair with fine grain. It would be less seemly to
howl, and yet I do howl now, inwardly. Or I could present myself
in the guise of the sunflower, black disc lolling in its autumnal
death throes. Forgive me for repeating myself, but it leaned over
my shoulder just then. It prompted me.

XCV

There is always such coarseness, everywhere. When they open
their mouths I see it, how their tongues, once so thick and so slow,
are now turned corrugated flashings of flame. I see it in their boots,
so slow and clod-hopping in their tedious, regular oncoming, and
those wheedling, sidelong glances. Coarseness everywhere, which
includes an unwillingness to acknowledge me. Which is exactly as it
should be, of course, because I myself consist of torn strips of
leather, still stinking from the tannery; loose scraps of paper,
random, unpremeditated, blowing about in the wind; and all
smoothed over with such washings of easy piety. It is I who have
made them coarse, by the example of my life. Once on a day they
were surely perfect. We were all surely perfect, and walking
together.

Too, too large again, by far, when I wake in the night. I perceive it with sudden alarm when I open my eyes, how my body is swelling out the very walls of this house – I hear the plaster beginning to crepitate; I see how the brickwork opens up, presenting the freezing night sky in the form of a hallowed gift. I hurry to fold myself into myself. I make the tiniest of balls of my hands, and quickly toss them elsewhere. It is good to be done with some part of me at least. Now they lie at the bottom of the garden, amongst the rotting crab apples, unnoticed. I lean forward with my upper body until it consists of two almost equal halves, one neatly stacked upon another. What I cannot control is the unruliness of my words. Each one spreads across the floor like a stain. I stuff my mouth with spilling handfuls of ash from the grate, but still I can hear my muffled murmurings, ever more desperate. I listen again. I prick up my ears in wonderment. I fear the joy that they give me, these words. And yet I have no wish to hear them. Even as they are uttered, they lie about themselves, so brazenly. They tell such a fantastic tale. They have no such submissiveness.

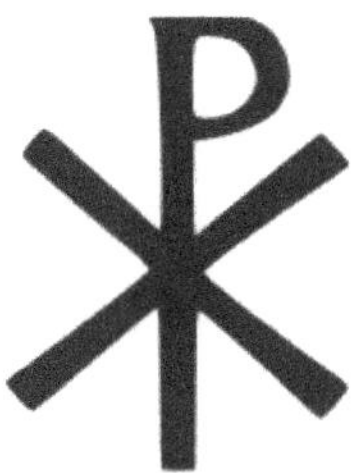

XCVII

Enfant docile,
Soumis à ses parents,
Leur humble asile
Pres d'eux le voit longtemps;
Par des travaux constants,
De ses plus tendres ans,
Dans un métier servile,
Il aide ses parents,
Enfant docile.

Let me sleep again for a little while, I ask again, as I am always asking. There has been too much of this daylight. I have surely mistaken daylight for everlastingness. It is always thus in the days of summer, when the light is so reluctant to withdraw itself, when the sun refuses to slip away into the density of that distant coppice, and I sit here in my seat, upright, pleading for the darkness to descend upon me. *O please do give me rest,* I whisper, over and over... I have no wish to dally with my ideas any more. Do I call them ideas? Am I pretending now to be another? Am I still endeavouring to walk in his footsteps? What is it that I am so eager to say to myself? What exactly is it that I amount to? Two finger pinches of oats perhaps, spilled out, in all carelessness, on this table top. I lean down to blow them away.

XCVIII

There is the peace of everything hereabouts. It is the peace of my noiseless dreams. It is also the peace of my wakefulness on this day, as I stand here like a pillar in the centre of this room, offering myself to the world, arms outspread. She comes then to dress me in my vestments, and I look askance as she does so. I feel her fingers upon me, fussing with my buttons, adjusting the regular flow of my whiteness, transforming me into a model of all earthly perfections. I would smile down at her if I could. I would thank her. I would even rummage in my inner pocket for a coin. But that is not my way. My way is to stand perfectly still and monumental in front of her, and to ask myself: in her mind, in her heart, does she admire me? Or does she despise me? She walks away from me with her small steps. She glances back at me, just the once, before she closes the door.

XCIX

Barrings of white crossed with barrings of black, and all spinning in front of my eyes until the brain begins to judder and the brow to break out in an unseemly sweat. Scenes of casual dismemberment: thin, helpless, childish arms, bruised and thickened legs, and a mass of individual organs of all sizes and conditions, strewn about wantonly. And then, to blink in helplessness, and to see these fields thrown across, once again, like an eye-soothing blanket, perfectly smooth at first, and then, little by little, undulating. Smooth as the unearthly singing which descends, down and down through the air, to lull me. There is a cure for all of this. A pinch of salt on the tongue, washed down with water, or held in a tiny heap in the mouth, at tongue's tip, projected just beyond the mouth so that it may be publicly acknowledged, by way of penance.

C

You are never here for me. I will you to be here. I say your name over and over until it dissolves into the meaninglessness of empty babble. I look into your face, but the eyes which would surely look back at me are absent. You have plucked them out. I have seen you slip them into your pocket in order to avoid looking back at me. And yet if you are not here, why must I always will you to be here, and why do you stand here in front of me when I close my eyes? Why are you still here with me when you are not here with

me? Why are you alive within me, why do you incandesce before me, when your body lies in the ground beside the sea, all limbs settled, arms folded, eyes closed fast shut? Why are the answers that you give to my questions not your answers? Why must I put words into your mouth? Why are you my final consolation? Why do you sit beside my bed at night, and lay your arms across me as if you are pledging to be my eternal companion? Are you, Paul, a liar and a jester after all?

CI

I have sought for an easier way, and there is no such way. I have dug a path for myself through the clay with my own hands. I have plotted the most serendipitous of routes through the lower marshlands, beside the river, where the cows are habitually browsing. I have consulted maps. I have hobnobbed with telegraph poles. And all have conspired to agree: there is no easier way. By the sweat of the brow. By the crawling upon all fours. By the utterance of words of a very special pleading, repeated and repeated until they scream back at you. In short, the steady walk that is never destined to end. The blankness – and the greyness – forever up ahead. This is the tale of the mighty hammer that will forever descend. This is the story of the sword that will slice off the head of the man who has been chosen to wield it.

CII

The anger of redness when the blood slow-oozes from the end of the finger is equal to the anger of her words when she stood above me and slapped me on the left cheek and then the right. I could do nothing then. I, a mere helpless child, had no anger stored within me. Everything was quite drained from me. I merely stood there, a small mannequin, waiting to be lifted and carried, quite roughly, and end on, into the corner of her sewing room, dark and dust-choked, where she would always store them, her mannequins, the best friends of her life, to whom she would mutter or whisper from time to time, pins clenched tight in teeth, fabric flapping in front of her, until she clothed them all again, and we were all humans together, though mute and unresisting.

CIII

This is the prison in which I have locked myself. I patrol its outer limits. I test its fastnesses. I am secure within it. It is the freedom of so little, the freedom to say yes to myself, the freedom to agree that all is as it should be, the freedom to face down my acts of intolerance, the freedom to know myself capaciously. I shall not be asking you to join me. You would be neither recognisable here nor welcome.

CIV

There is loss. There is also gain. Even as I shrink and fall away from myself, I am increasing, I am growing. The earth has not given up on me. It dutifully sustains me. It prepares reports about my activities from beyond the window. It peers in at me, ever curious. I do not want its curiosity. I want everything about me to be unpremeditated. Sudden burstings out. Quick efflorescences. That way I impress myself. I applaud myself. I take some pride in being my best and only audience. I ask to see all over again everything that I have always been. I reward myself, bountifully, for my exploits. I kiss my own cheeks. I identify myself as the saviour of this tiny sliver of mankind.

CV

To divide a morsel into ever finer dicings, and to feed each one to
my boon companion, that fat, drunken spider, suspending it from a
corner of its web until it sways and jounces below the ceiling. The
cracklings and the creakings and the roarings of oncoming daylight,
and how I rush towards it, eager to eat and be eaten by this
daysong. The grass blades have narrowed and keened. I hear their
keen-bladed delivery beyond the window. I whistle through them.
Meanwhile, good neighbourliness hangs and swags hereabouts like
a sullen cloud. And, once again, I am at my ablutions, removing
every last scrap of unnecessary skin from my body, paring myself
back to the bone. Now there is nowhere for me to hide from
myself.

CVI

Many lacklustre days. Many separate moments of dying appeal.
Many slow and turgid remembrances. Which is why I call it a good
thing to do away with all falsehoods of memory, to be entirely rid
of that burden. Now I have no way of anticipating my own misery. I
have never had the acquaintance of such a word. A great loosening
and outblaring – as of a flock of skyborne bassoons – everywhere
approaches. I fall into my future. I fall just as far as my body will
take me, with all its fleas still clinging so helplessly. Even as I spin
and dive so plungingly, I crack my fleas between thumb and finger.
I count them even as they swim away from me.

CVII

Not nothing forever. Or perhaps not something. Or all points in-
between. The abiding curse of all that. The saying it over and over,
and then the harsh refusal to do so. Turning away the head. Staring
fiercely at floor, ceiling, boots. Certain easy repetitions to soothe

away care. Oooooh. Oooooh. And perhaps to say: never here again. And yet still to be here again. To be always and forever here. Contemplating the illusion of elsewhere, to be lifted there, enraptured, on the wings of the moment, and to be perfectly at ease on that flight, as if in an airborne armchair. All this is so much torment to me, this passing through the day, with nothing behind me and nothing ahead of me, and Paul, lips pursed, in the corner, the spider's corner, aglow in all his respectability. If I were to touch him, if I were to inch that far out of myself, he would surely shatter, such is his exquisite fragility.

CVIII

Night will forever show its grievances, its open wounds. It is there that the past enlivens itself. The dead ones come flocking then, all of a-twitter, all agog, to play with me. They show me to myself as I would wish to be, a seamless garment. They offer up to me tableaux of my childhood, flickerings, evanescent flickerings, always evanescent. Nothing endures for too long. There is always, as twilight comes on, easing its way between us, the return to the end of the jetty. The slop, the staring down, to the fathomless, slow-heaving black. The terminus. No, nothing endures for too long. I am carried away like a lumpish sack, howling. I can never stop myself thirsting for such magic. If only I could (just now, you will understand) be still, inert, heavy and opaque, unbudgeable, as any fond stone in this garden. Then I could so easily be cherished, carried above their heads, acknowledged to be everything that is not precisely anything. It is too precious to be questioned, too distant, too high-raised. That is where I would be, in those lofty, wind-chilled spaces, between the eaves, between the stars, nudging fondly at the outer galaxies. Certainly not here, not now.

CIX

Today, in all my headlong rashness, I swept out of the door random gustings of a terrible coldness, and it has now returned, as if to admonish me for my failures of perceptiveness. Having sat still here for an hour or two, hands pressed close between bony knees, rocking, bent forward like a strung bow stretched to its uttermost limits, I now understand the manifold reasons for its return. I am in essence that coldness. It is my guardian and my guide. It is everything that I need – and everything that I would desire – to guide me through this life. Much worse would be to warm and to bend and to melt and then to spill – or to slop – parts of myself hither and thither, across the floors of this room or in the hedgerows. Slathered there like so much stinking pig muck. The only way to keep a firm grip upon the self is to cleave to the ice of one's essence. It is to be feared. It is not readily to be approached. One need not live in fear of vulnerability. Let vulnerability ever continue to stalk beyond these walls, night and day, unsleeping. And, thankfully, barely audible at all when the self is neatly slotted beneath the blanket, almost sleeping, almost at rest.

CX

Peace is the quick descent of the hammer, at such a time, almost certainly, when the body is sporting itself out of doors, unwittingly, making some pretence at frolicsome youthfulness. It is then that the hammer will descend, and there will be no further questions. What then will come after? The peace of a great and forever outstretching blankness. Grey? Green? Or what? Some hue hitherto unknown or unknowable? And no people, certainly. No clamour. No hubbub. No laughter. No voices for laughter. Perhaps a gentle soughing of sorts, barely discernible – like a small wind beneath the door. You roll up the cloth to block it, and still it finds its way, ever wheedlingly persistent. There is always that slight fear of the wind, and the way it has of finding its way in.

CXI

Where then is the way of things this morning? Am I to be cracked open like the shell of an egg, and wholly exposed? Is it the narrow way today? Or is it to be the broad way and the green? There is no one here to tell me. No words approach me through these walls, no words of a certain soothingness. I have always waited in vain for such a thing. Hundred of hours – perhaps thousands, who knows? – I have patiently waited. I have been contented to wait, let there be no bones about it, like some dumb, browsing beast in a sty, turning and turning in its ordure, and not once remarking upon its predicament. Is that who – or what – I have been? Can there never be any response to this question? Are these walls, to which I have always been so faithful, not ready to give me something in return? The smallest gesture of clemency perhaps? Will these walls, in time, not sweat for me? Will these walls, after all, not find themselves guilty of feeling?

CXII

Yes, she said. And then, no, no, no again, showing me the flat of her hand, at which I would turn away, swivelling my narrow head like a quick-turning screw, and yet still knowing in my heart of hearts the solemn aftermath. And as I stared at that hand of hers, I would say: I am liquid today. Her hand will pass straight through me. After the end of things, there will surely be a new beginning. There will be no end to the flow of water, the movement of water from its source in the abundance of nature.

CXIII

I had a dream, and it so shocked me that I lay trembling in my bed, crooning with pleasure. The sun had entered my heart, with all its life-giving heat. I had been lying there in my cot, in the outer dark, cold and inert as a stone, and then, without warning, the sun had come bowling, down down through the upper air, towards me until, jumping, it planted itself deep in the chambers of my heart. And there its heat, the heat of its radiance, revived and sustained me. I had been staring at myself for such long hours, knowing the doleful truth of the cadaver that I had become, and I had been mourning my loss with such tears and stamping and long words of lamentation. And then, all of a sudden, this had happened, this transformation, this bolt of good fortune. The sun now sat in the midst of my heart like a mother hen brooding upon its egg, and my heart had woken up and crowed out loud in its pleasure, in the pleasure of such a release, back into the world of men, where I live now with such displeasure. That is the worst of it all. Every blessing drags behind it in its wake entire worlds of sorrow.

CXIV

Paul is calling to me now from across the waters. He is waving to me, as if everything in this world must always be so urgent. Although the two of us are so wide-divided, one from another, that great, slow-moving hand of his is agitating in my direction, and I am of course responding. I cannot believe that he wants me. Can he really want me? Or need me? Surely he cannot need me. And yet what is there to be done? He is on that shore, and I am on this one. What is more, the shore on which I stand is flooded with light, and the light-bearers are huddled around me, a great mass of them, protectively. I need nothing more than this light, I have been thinking, over and over. All this is more than sufficient. And then he, Paul, comes calling, from across the waters. I raise both arms to him. I give him my semaphore of welcome, o welcome, and he undoubtedly sees me. But his shoreline is in darkness, and he stands alone, entirely helpless, whereas mine is light-flooded and, what is more, the waters between us are still rising and rising. There is such an anger in these waters, I am thinking.

CXV

Coldness. Scorn. Pity. I take each one out of its box in turn, and subject it to tight, fierce, ever closer scrutiny. I fear pity most of all because it is so soft and so wheedling. I feel it worming its way beneath my skin, with its very special pleading. Its voice, so light-timbred, disgusts me. Coldness can be repelled with a quick flick of the hand or a stare of such unimpeachable *froideur* that it knows, immediately, that I give like for like, and retires into its box without protestation. Scorn growls in the air, neck muscles fully distended. I watch how it faces the wall, shadow-boxing so fiercely with itself. There is no question of any intervention. I walk away, calmly, weighing my own footfalls, feeling, on the back of my neck, how it stares and stares after.

CXVI

My birthing was the event of my life. I participated with a lively degree of attentiveness. I cheered at the blood with which I was smearing myself as I rushed helter-skeltering down the birth canal towards the light of my being. And then it all stopped for me. It was my first and my last event. What I saw I knew I did not want. It repulsed me. I turned my back on my new life, that promise of a new openness to the caterwauling of the light. I tried to clamber backwards, splashing about as I slipped and I slid, back up into the darkness of the canal. But it would not have me. The doors were closed upon me. A great lock of such and such a heft had been fitted, and the key deep-swallowed forever. Of such is my misery.

CXVII

To sip at the morning light. Or to spue it out, in horror. The choices. The inevitable choices. I ask for no less.

CXVIII

These are my possibilities as day pursues day with a relentless tedium. The where and the what and the who and the why and the whither and the wheretofore, forever. Or finger-pointing beside the road. Or staring up directly into the gulf of the sky, limitless, nothing to stop the eye's foolish, idle journeyings to the where and the who and the whither. Or feeling on the dry finger tips the flimsy, makeshift back of things. Or reaching out in the dark – outer or inner? – towards the bedside table, and finding the dear hand, the waiting hand of a dear mother or a dear father or a dear neighbour – were there such hereabouts. Or clutching the coldness of a smoothly rounded pebble. To knead that instead, for minutes on end, urging warmth into it. A hopeless task. Who has ever warmed a pebble? Who but a god has ever warmed a pebble?

CXIX

Here beside – some momentary flicker of movement – and then oh so rapidly away again. The human warmth of breath near the coverlet, breasting it – did I once feel it on my skin, when I so gingerly touched it, was that how I understood it? – and then, when I came to open my eyes, to see that familiar yellow staining on the upper wall next to the window which overlooks the sullen blankness of the rooftops. Senseless to make any effort to move the body. Altogether far too heavy in its semi-somnolence. The settled aroma of its bed-bound unbudgeability. This is all for the best, surely. This is all for the best, now and forever.

CXX

The rat-a-tat-tattings of the drum in the hollow of the left palm. That pulsing. That ever-onward, violent pulsing. The entire bed trembling apprehensively. Who am I to be? Who am I to become? I measure myself, using means rough and ready: my fingers' span. Smaller still. And yet smaller. Then lifted and weighed. Preyed upon. Flung up in the air, tumbling head over heels, like a child's rag doll. Or tossed aside into some lightless corner, forgotten. The task is to burrow deep down, deeper than deep, and then you will not be lonely. I have written those words to myself in this letter that I am once again re-reading. Hourly. It is a form of medication, you must surely understand.

CXXI

This is as much as I would wish to say. And I have said it. On such a day. At such an hour. The outburst. And, later, all the down-falling consequences, over the months and the years, of this great survival. Having grown into myself, for example. Taking the body to task, in its entirety, finger end to crown of head, to heel. Tearing off strips and snatches. Adding particular patches, carefully, in order to disguise all the bruisings and the rendings. Self-presentation again, in courtyard, kitchen or parlour, as boy or man or stevedore or butler. Practically anything, in fact. Anything of weight and moment, anything with a modicum of solidity. Anything that, when pushed, will not readily fall over. A dream, in short, with all lights blazing.

CXXII

What have I asked of myself? Must I say it again in order to convince you – by which I mean convince myself? There was a short walk that I promised to undertake, weaving between the flower beds, with the light always fading. Was that sufficient? Did I prove myself by it? The box was duly ticked. I passed on by a little later, in full sail, and you were said to have acknowledged me.

CXXIII

This mechanism is so boundlessly pleasing. How the arm rises and falls when the lips demand wine or water. How the legs swivel down from the bed and carry the body hither and thither without overmuch protestation. These are all my bits and pieces, and I feel inclined to kneel and to praise them for doing my every bidding. It is so rare to brim over like this. Why are the clouds not louring? I know myself to be a man without ambition.

CXXIV

I walk to the outer limits of myself. I am still there, looking back at myself, forever haunted and haunting, forever quizzical. I am sucked back to the moment of my birth. I see myself appearing, pouring down that chute in all my bloody majesty, eyes tight screwed against the light, piping and groaning. The truth of it is this: I am never not present to myself. There is no escaping the burden of this self, so wretched, so incommensurable. I am this lumpish sack at my elbow. I am the heaped earth beneath my feet. I am this cloud which lours over me. Helpless, utterly helpless. Forever doomed to repeat myself, no matter in which direction I happen to be looking, to be this infinite series of eternal mirrorings. Where must I go then to be rid of it all? Can there be an answer to this, that I am always standing there, patiently waiting, at the ends of the earth, arms outspread, so ready and so eager to receive myself?

CXXV

This morning I said to myself: go. And I did not go. I did not obey my own commandment. I lay in the dark, stretched tight as a string, in a mood of bloody defiance. I spoke once again to myself, and still I chose not to listen. I feigned deafness, an outrageous deafness. I felt proud then of the extent of my wilfulness. It was no small indication of my manly character. And then a great and muffling silence began to fall about me. I was wrapped in it, and to such an extent that I found it almost impossible to breathe, let alone squirm. I tried to speak then, to explain, to apologise for my obstinacy, my obduracy. But there was no one there to listen. They had all gone away. They had all turned their backs on me. They were attending to the business of the world. How long? How long? I kept on asking myself. And then a voice began to speak to me, a voice other than my own voice, a voice that was beckoning me to stand now on my two feet. And then I threw off that cloud of unknowing, and I stood again, just so, in all my comely youthfulness. I even danced a little, first one leg raised and then the other, to give myself pleasure. It was not my own voice, that voice which had called me. And yet it was my voice, because that voice and I, we were quite inseparable. Surely.

CXXVI

The shrivelled pith or kernel. To be spat out, sieved through the teeth, swallowed. Contemptible. Ground beneath the heel until it is practically nothing at all. Just as I am nothing at all on those days, so many, so slow and sultry, when I am not everything. And I must be everything because I am everything to myself, and there is nothing to be touched or savoured beyond me. This all, it is all in the touching and the savouring. It is only there in so far as I absorb it all into myself. I am therefore everything to myself. I am as much as I can ever be, which inclines me towards a degree of swellheadedness. Until I notice that I am nothing again, when disabling doubt or conscience stings me, and then I shrink myself to almost nothing, to this shrivelled pith or kernel of sorts, to be spat out, sieved through the teeth or swallowed, or ground beneath the heel until I am nothing at all.

CXXVII

Listen to me with patience and understanding, if you would oblige me. I take this walk down to the *Lavoir*. It is my daily burden. I would not be without it. I count my own footsteps as I go. I seldom look up as I slow-foot it. I smell cow-reek in the meadow. I see beside the *chemin* – my foot grazes against it – a heap of tumbled stones where a labourer's cottage is falling into ruin. I watch the gentle, regular sway of the cassock as it polishes the edge of my black boot. And on I go, usually when the light is falling, during the stark, crepuscular light of evening, and I have no need of anyone to watch over me because I am watching over myself, in all my brittleness and my cowardly tentativeness, amidst the ponderous grind of my wits'-dulling anxiety. All those characteristics range themselves around me like a burdensome cloak of office. Consequently I have no need of anything or anyone else. And, needless to say, no one greets me or interrupts me or warmly salutes me because, frankly, I am not a man of that character. Mud does not bother me. Fine rain needling the eyelids does not impede me. All I know is that I must take myself there – it is a kind of summons – to see once again the *Lavoir*, at the bottom of the village, that place where they go to wash their clothes in the morning – at that hour most often. Needless to say, there is no one present when I choose to make my visit, I have made sure of that by the lateness of this hour. Do I see the imprint of their heavy bodies on the stone slabs that surround that rectangle of water? No I do not. Do I half-hear some faint after-echo of their idle chatter, their whisperings, their laughter, their daily confidences? No I do

not. Do I even see her there afloat on the water, face down? No, I do not. I see nothing. I know nothing. I return to my house once again, in silence. I rid my mind of everything. It is an empty vessel.

CXXVIII

Everything that I am said to know perhaps I do not know. How in the world does this old chair continue to support me when I am so undeserving? How does the light win me every passing new morning, as if beckoning me to rise? How do these vain thoughts give me passing succour? There will surely come a day when this bowl will fly from my hand as I am about to take that first sip of my morning coffee. It will spin away from me into the air, and I will be powerless to stop it. There will come a day when this food – such as it is – will writhe in front of my face in a small, compacted mass, and taunt me when I try to catch it. It will be useless then to point at my mouth. What is a mouth for? those mouthfuls of food will chorus back at me. There will come a day when these books will have lost all their characters. Each and every letter will have crept away from its page and, single file, they will all stream away from me, and I will be watching them, angered, frustrated and ashamed, as they walk their miles and miles to the library of some other such as I, a fortunate newcomer to the lively life of the mind, who even now inhabits his own comfortable dream of the solidity of the world in some other village, so little different in every way from this one.

CXXIX

I call it peace, but it is a not-peace. It is a terrible standing still, a refusal to budge from this place, a refusal to accept anything other than this particular species of rootedness. Rootedness, then, as a kind of rottenness. How the very words seem to cleave to each other, to echo one another! This is a very shallow kind of soil, barely a soil at all, in which I have chosen to root myself. Strewn stones across strata of rock, that is the truth of it. *Galets.* No wonder that my standing is always so precarious. No wonder that I know myself to be leaning and leaning when they regard me as upright, facing them. No wonder that they do not see me, the truth of me, almost falling forwards into their uncomprehending arms. It is much as I can do to hold myself upright at such times. It is a kind of feigning.

CXXX

Just there, and nowhere else, where you stood at that hour. And where I saw you as standing. There was no doubting you. There was no doubting the fetid, looming presence of your body. There was no saying to myself (as I might have said of myself): no, not at all. And you will surely always be there, re-enacting all those careful acts of encirclement. I would hold you with my eye at such times as those, furiously, though you would never see me. I would say yes and yes to you. I would say: you and not I, inevitably. My paper-thinness beside your solidity. My flimsiness beside your rock-hardness. To be blown free or tossed aside. To be summarily disregarded. To be passed on by. Whereas you, you lived in my presence there for the purpose of blocking the light. You stood four-square in front of me. You consisted of a certain indomitable, unassailable assurance. You thickened the very air around you. Words, mere words, fell away from you. No words could be your equal. I circumnavigated you in a drifting wonder, nodding as I went, all infantine, bibbly-babbly foolishness.

CXXXI

Strike it all out again. Now. Without a second's hesitation. Stir yourself from this poisonous reverie. Too incomplete. Too inadequate. Nothing at all as I have written it. All the formulations inadequate, as Paul would be the first to remind me. Trust not to memory, he would say, the waywardness, the speciousness, the volatility of memory. To remember is to show too much kindness to Dame Falsehood. Do not invite her to sit beside your hearth, winding her hands. Take this cork and stopper up her mouth because it will all be so lullingly seductive, the much that she will have to tell you, the shocking green spue from her mouth. Clap your palms to your ears. Never fail to remember: you were not as you once were. There is no story to be told, no tale worthy of the eager, flap-eared, dolt-like listener. Think of the glass and how it once shattered at your feet. Think of how the fragment lodged in the eye. The truth lies in all that painful misting over.

CXXXII

This is my everlasting burden, as he once reminded me on that day, so long ago when, in all my vaingloriousness, I chose not to heed his words: the fear of endlessness. No end to the aftermath of the decline of the body, when all begins to fall away: hand reducing to a slither of flesh across the smooth swell of bony knuckles; teeth rattling around inside the mouth's dry cavern as if they belonged elsewhere; legs withered to the condition of brittle sticks fit only for the flames. This, alas, is the merest beginning of all human suffering. Worse still will be the burden of the spirit's immortality, when night and day it will be prowling, ceaselessly, hither and thither, striving, imperfectly, to fend off the ghostly recollections of life's ceaseless humiliations, when we climbed and we climbed before falling back, when our answers, such as they were, went always unheeded. The head hammering upon the boards of the door, forehead to wood, again and again, and never gaining admittance.

CXXXIII

Did I ask you then to lodge an appeal on my behalf? There was a moment, yesterday or thereabouts, when I stood on the topmost step of the house, door thrown back to admit the freshness of new morning, waiting to ask you, of that I have little doubt. Were you there at all? Had you already been and gone? No matter. What mattered was the vehemence of my purpose. The words were on my lips. They were bursting forth. Gushing like a stream in spring. An appeal. Against these circumstances in which I never cease to find myself. Lodged here, fast, like a stake of wood driven into the cloggy earth at the corner of this graveyard just beyond the perimeter of the house, by no one, and for no particular reason. A stake of wood of such and such a height, barely noticed. Occasionally stumbled over. And the appeal itself? It was a plea perhaps for my removal. It was a plea for my transportation. It was a plea for me to be carried away, to the carpenter's shop, so that I could be whittled away, shaved and trimmed just so, until something else became of me. Something lustrous or useful perhaps. Or not. A splinter in the eye. A dust mote. A match stick. To give flame. To encourage, by means of a sudden, unearthly sputter (I see it now), all that oncoming brightness. So quick. So passing.

CXXXIV

Mine then – who else's, in heaven's name? – are all these futile mouthings. No one else's. You need not have asked that question. Mine then was all the casual gathering of these words from hither and thither, such carelessly approximate concatenations and collidings, futile, ear-grating percussionings. My head is full of empty-headedness, now and forever more. I see it all, streaming away. Floating above itself, like a dream of nothing at all. It will never take hold. It will always be there, idly drifting away from me.

I call to it. It does not heed me. I beckon. It turns away. It does not recognise its own name. This uncomprehending, self-accusatory solitariness, in which nothing must always buffet against nothing, and I have become my own indifferent neighbour to myself, shrugging, passing by on the other side, knowing that there is nothing to be known.

CXXXV

I have been looking for myself everywhere, as child or man. It has been a matter of indifference to me whether child or man, surprising though that may seem to you. I have been hearing these words of urgent interrogation: where in the world did you find me? It is one child asking another, with a hiss of urgency, as if the voice cannot quite believe that it has been chanced upon, in that tumbled heap, unwashed, unloved, unrecognised. And then comes the moment of discovery, when the throat cannot but choke on its own words, and those words are uttered, as if from nowhere and to no one: found me. You have surely found me. And it raises its head from the ground – so heavy a head, whether young or old – and blinks awake at last, having slept that sleep of hundreds of years. Or of no time at all. Who is there to say how long the sleeper sleeps if there is no one there to observe and record? And so it was with me this morning, when I raised my head from the bed's head beside the window, just inches from those oh so familiar cobwebby interlacings, and heard myself saying, as if prompted by some curious voice, in a voice – surely my own? – which sounded so strange to myself. Yes, mine was surely that stranger's voice, high and strangulated, that needy child's voice, and it was saying, as if to some other: where in the world did you find me? And as I listened to that voice, I said to myself: were you in fact there to be found? Can there be truth in it? Surely you were not there to be found. Surely you are mistaken. You are a blankness. You have been erased long ago. There was no child to be father to the man. You have slipped sidelong into falsehood. There is no imprint. It is simply not there to be discovered.

CXXXVI

I stack them beside each other in the sink: bowl, cup, spoon. Cup. Spoon. Bowl. I am saying the words out loud to myself as I lower them into the engulfing shadows of that deep porcelain sink, with all its painful marks of ageing – the craquelure of its surface, its melancholy stainings, for example. I raise each one back up to the light of new morning, in my two ancient and dependable hands. Very slowly. Very deliberately. Very ritualistically. I have watched her from the table, time out of mind, how she has dealt with them – not well, not well – as if they are objects of scant importance, how she has carelessly clashed them against each other like a red-faced child with its cymbals. I have wanted to close my ears against all the careless racket that she is making, against all the bustle and the unseemly hurry, all those bodily blunderings. I have wanted to rise up, quiet and composed as a ghost, from my chair at the table, and tap her, quite gently, on the roundedness of her shoulder, and advise her, quite calmly and collectedly, to slow down, slow down, please slow down. I have wanted to say to her: there is such a gravity and a solemnity associated with the oft used things of this world. They are not to be treated lightly, as if they might come and go, without pain or suffering. They too are inclined to suffer, even as we ourselves contemplate their suffering. Which is why I raise each one up in its turn from the sink each and every morning, treating them with all due reverence, and the spoon first of all, smiling back at its friendly gleam, in acknowledgement of how it offers me, so freely and so willingly, my daily sustenance of high piled grain and milk, the milk brimming over and, occasionally, even spilling before it enters the mouth. And how the bowl then catches it as it falls, pittery-pattering down upon the surface of the grain like so much rain falling down from the sky, cleansing and brightening to a high-gleaming greenness those fat tussocks of grass in the graveyard, or causing the hollyhocks, those doughty two or three, to stand tall just beyond the kitchen window, my bravest of brave sentinels, which I salute every morning in order to give myself a small jolt of wholly unanticipated pleasure.

CXXXVII

When all turns intolerable again to both eye and mind, as it did just moments ago, when I found myself twisting my neck at the head of the stairs, and facing down, down into the gulf of the air, I remind myself once again that it is good to be absent from here, to say goodbye to it all, albeit fondly and even wistfully. I am such a fool. Say it now. No hesitations. To strip the walls from the walls as one would scarify the body – Marsyas upended, for example – so that I am once again eager to see – yes, it represents a great freshening of the eye – through to all the yawning opennesses of this new day's helpless oncoming, even though the day itself is so cold and so inclement for the time of year. And what exactly is the time of year? Has somber-suited November returned yet again, and so soon? Can that really be true? Yes, I look again beyond this window, and I see that I am here for no particular purpose, and that it is right then to strip it all away, all this thin veneer of purposefulness, all this empty, world-consuming, world-defining bustle and heave, as if this house and all the things of this house were tailored to the needs of doltish man and his incessant blunderings. And it is all true, of course. Who could doubt it? There is no other reason for the existence of this house. No other species of worm would have thought to build it. I stand here, arms outspread, ready to be lifted, oiled, knotted and tethered, with nothing but myself to blame for it all. Life is this catalogue of oncoming chastisements. I walk steadily towards it. There is no other way.

CXXXVIII

You appear in the lane on no particular day, granted. Nosing forward in the direction of the gate, head bowed, like something wild and untameable. And yet you are always so mild-mannered. What is more, it is all so seemingly haphazard, the way of you, what you do here, and what you are to me. And let us leave it that way. What is more, I have never asked for you to appear in front of me as if we were about to engage in some form of colloquy. I am beyond the need of conversation. Nothing outward will breeze in to correct me. It is the self alone which schemes and calculates, and that is exactly how it should be. Its calculations consist of inward ruminations, internal echoings. The thisness of me, that is what I most seek to know. My end and my beginning. The extent of my borderlands. The wildest of my hinterlands. My sea-borne voyagings. What I throw I must also receive back. It is a game forever in the playing. I am perpetually readying myself for the contest. My vocabulary is quite sufficient and up to the minute. Keenly honed. How and from where I gathered it? Ask me if you wish. And then trouble to listen to my answer. Let me say this: it suffices me to dice finely. Ever more finely. You may not see me. Most certainly you will never hear me because I so seldom speak. There is so little beyond the smallness that is me. That is why I am entirely sufficient. My littleness is also my grandeur, my invisible grandeur. My littleness is also the world's grandeur. To see myself is always more than sufficient. I fill this space of my life. From time to time I am even straining at my seams. I calm myself a little from time to time. I take myself to my bed in order to calm myself. I measure it, quite obsessively: how many breaths to the minute.

CXXXIX

God. Oh God. The incessant beating of a hollow drum. The most terrible of thuddings, repeated, and then again repeated until the very earth reverberates beneath the feet. A mighty stone, quick to pulverise. And then to rise from the ground, dazed, wrapped in all the majesty of the kingdom of death. Does it still fill me to the brim like a pitcher brimming over? Do I still run headlong towards it, so eager and willing to crawl through its interstices? Or do I crawl away from it, on all fours, licking the wounds of my humiliation? Does it shrink me to a nothing at all, robbing me of all speech, all meaningful action? And what of meaning itself? Consider this question: how do I love you? Where is the meaning in this? It is to throw kisses at the empty air, to embrace the wind. I once saw myself seeing so clearly, to the outermost limits of the universe, in all my fine, uptowering hubris. Then I grew smaller and smaller. I see less and less, and the little that I see consists of these words that I use, which are entirely within the scope of my manipulation. These words are my kingdom. I have built this kingdom. And now I am tearing it down with my own bare hands.

CXL

This clock has not yet said a single word to me. Not yet. In fact, this clock has not uttered a word. Instead, it has always attended to its own sober habits, which consist of nothing but dutifulness, regularity, dependability. This clock, in short, is always so timely. It knows how much I prize it for these things, how often I stare into its face at times of doubt or sorrow or bemusement or unknowing. It knows that I wish to be able to say to myself: ah yes, it is such and such an hour again, as it was yesterday. I reckon up and I fill each one of my passing moments as a pitcher is filled to the brim, so carefully, with water from a well. I try not even to consider the possibility of the blankness or the emptiness of my moments. And this clock, so attentive beside my bed here, helps me to anticipate, with a measure of sober calmness, exactly what will become of me. It helps me to describe a future for myself as any cartographer might map an unknown country. It enables me to whisper as I breathe, leaning forward and often squinting, into its face: as was today, so will be tomorrow. As was today, so will be tomorrow. Nothing more could be asked of this life. This clock of mine is sufficient unto the day. It will never not heed me and attend to my every need, from the hour of my waking to the hour of my passing away.

CXLI

I have scored myself through. I have taken up this pen, and I have made the most violent of erasures, again and again. The fact is that I am going nowhere – I am listing and I am drifting like a rudderless boat – and it has always been so. There has been a simulacrum of movement down the days, the weeks, the months, the years, but when I do my best to close-scrutinise exactly how far I have travelled, I find no credible evidence that I have taken even a single step. I am playing the same few dull tunes that I have always played. Or perhaps the same dull tune. Why boast that there is more than one? My mind has arrived at the very point in the journey from which it started. I stare at this thin shell of an idea that I call an idea, and I see nothing but nothing. I am a subject and an object of the utmost futility. I have added nothing to the sum of myself. I have listened to my own heart beating. I have walked from my bed to the head of the stairs, and then stared down. I have walked from window to door, and then back again. I have filled this spoon that I currently hold between finger and thumb full to the brim with salt, and I have touched my tongue to it. Sharpness. Bitterness. Disgust.

CXLII

And then, without any warning, you made me this gift of the box. You left it on the threshold, just beyond the door, and this morning I found it. In fact, I almost stumbled over it. I lifted it into the

kitchen – it was not especially heavy – with all due ceremony. I felt a sudden spasm of delight that you should have done such a thing. I myself have never made such a gift. Have I received one? Not within living memory. I cleared the table of a great number of my books, making a space just sufficient, and then I sat down and I stared at it. Something deep within me took such pleasure in the contemplation of what exactly it might contain. My fingers ached to open it, and I prevented them from doing so for minutes on end by saying out loud: be patient. It will arrive soon enough. And then, in the late afternoon, just as the light was falling, I prised off the lid. Now I have you. Now you have arrived here.

CXLIII

What could be more apposite, more faithful to the temper of the hour, than the closing of this book on my knee? It is good to be rid of such interruptions. I know books which have robbed me of my dignity. I know books which have led me astray. I know books which have said to me, in a tone not far short of peremptory: go here. And I have gone there, and it was the wrong destination. As soon as I arrived, I understood, with horror, that I had lost myself. And so I have closed this book today – there will be other days, other hours, when it will sing again sweetly to me – in order to allow myself as much time as I need today – will it be two hours or three or more? – to wander around inside myself, wonderingly, and even a little apprehensively, and say: this is a little like drifting through empty and long abandoned rooms. There are signs of life to be looked out for. There are objects, barely recognisable now, which still stare back at me as if I am likely to be causing an affront by engaging them with my eye. Calming myself, I move through different vistas, different moods. Not all the flowers are dead. Some have even woken, and raised their heavy heads, and are singing now in anticipation of my imminent approach.

CXLIV

At dawn, on a day such as this one, daylight sifts down through the air, grainily, indistinctly, scarcely knowable at all. The eye opens in near disbelief that the world has begun again. Can it really be happening all over again, this new day? Must life always consist of the dull, interminable rhythms of new day, followed yet again by new day? Is life itself a hopeless, Sisyphean labour? I raise my right hand – as in that schoolroom long ago – to let its veins catch the faint light. The light scarcely adheres to it. It is so timid at this hour. The truth is that I can barely see myself. I can barely feel myself beneath the blanket. Am I really this insubstantial? Do I fade, daily? My legs make a few small animal scurryings, as if to reassure me. Inner knee rubs against bald inner knee. My mouth yawns open to take in dust and air. My eyes are afflicted by such a soreness. I go to rub them with my knuckles. And still it comes on at me, in spite of all, the new light of a new day, in all its slow and tentative brightening. I twist my head in order to examine it through the window, yet again, as at every other dawn hour, the great, heaving bulk of that church, its massiness. The stones are almost alive this morning. They seem to be shifting, and even writhing, a little in their deep moorings. It is near-darkness which conjures such imaginings from deep within me, and which causes those stones, weighted one upon another, each one of a heft sufficient to crush a human hand, to feel almost alive within me, alive with anticipation. Of what exactly? When the sun floods the stones at a later hour than this, they will return to their customary state of silent, slow, unbudgeable, dependably compacted solidity, but for now the world is a different place altogether, more slippery and more alarming to my gaze. At a later hour than this one, the church will not dare to move. The pitiless glare of full daylight will have it in a fierce grip.

CXLV

I have been reached before. No, approached. I forget exactly when. In the early years. I remember the footsteps, and how tentative they were the closer they came to me. There was a certain magnetism in the air that morning, it cannot be denied. I could see that it was happening – I always keep one eye open for surprises, even when I pretend to be paying no attention – I could see the hand upon the gate, and how the head bowed in acknowledgement of the fact that something difficult was about to be attempted – or accomplished. I dipped my head beneath the window sill in order to absent myself. I crawled on all fours across the kitchen floor, as nimble and quick-moving as a kitten. I mounted the steep stairs. I gained the upper chamber, from where I could watch him, hesitating again, taking in this and that, as he moved across the garden towards the flight of steps which ascends to the door. I could have asked myself whether I knew the man, whether I had ever seen him about the village. And then I listened for his knock on the door. I assessed its weight, its authority. I counted the length of the pause before he raised the knocker once again. There was a considerable pause, sufficient to make the heart pound. Then I watched him as he slowly retired. Hesitant once again, a trifle puzzled. Having left the garden, he did not once look back. Was I to regard that as significant or not? No, here was the matter of true significance: that he had left me, and I could cleave to myself once again. All was free again, unbounded.

CXLVI

My life consists of... how much exactly? Or is that, finally, unknowable? Could it be contained, say, within a single sack? And what proportion of the contents of that sack might consist of these words of mine, no matter how worthless or unruly? And how many words are there exactly? Could they be counted? Words fall out in

a very particular order, and there are many such orders. What is more, I can use the same word, often, to mean something quite different. I lean heavily upon a word, or I increase its musicality when spoken out loud. Each reality is quite different. And then, when I come to be reduced to dust in the end, a heap of scattered ashes, what exactly will remain of me and of all those words of mine? Nothing, I sincerely hope. But is that possible? Are there not those who will remember the least little thing about me, and especially my disgusting foibles? Can I really tidy myself away so that nothing at all remains of me? Can I bring about a situation in which I am entirely forgotten? When even my name is forgotten? That is why I have not told you my name, so that you will forever lack that useful handle.

CXLVII

A box – this box, the one she left beside the window – represents useful containment. It is a way of managing the superfluities, the incongruities of the body, with all its needless sprawl, its comic gaucheness, its random spillage. Yes, to collapse, deflate, dismantle the body in some way, and then, having done so, to live within the dark and straitening confines of this box, comfortably, comfortingly. Would that not be the sweetest of my ideals? And then to stow the box on a high shelf – how though? – on the topmost shelf of the *armoire* perhaps, and to live within it, unmoving, scarcely breathing, in fact slowly counting the breaths as a species of lulling diversion, for days, weeks and even months at a time. Utterly, magnificently self-sufficient, utterly elsewhere within its confining walls, transporting the spirit goodness knows where, whilst, at the same time, remaining utterly still, utterly sequestered, unbudging. That would be my desire. Quite impossible, of course, to shrink to such a size, to deprive oneself of one's daily sustenance. How we howl like animals for the daily allotment of food! The fingers must always be reaching out for it, the solace of food. We must always be staring at the grease on our finger tips. How our hands ache to knit themselves, in the dreamy aftermath of all that bestial gorging, across the pleasing breadth of the swollen stomach.

CXLVIII

In the night, as on so many other nights, she came to me again, crowding around me, just the one of her again, yet seeming, as before, so many; all those faces, and yet always the same face, as if repeated, infinitely, in a mirror. Was I asleep or was I waking? Yes, in the night she came to me again, saying this or that – I scarcely know what exactly – with such ferocity, shouting the words directly into my face, as if she wished to destroy, outright, eyes, nose, teeth, ears, everything about me. I flinched. I screwed up my eyes. I tried to twist my face away from her. I even thought I tried to run. I had the impulse to run, certainly, I punched out with my legs, certainly, but it was quite impossible. I was locked in my bed, in sleep perhaps, part-dreaming perhaps. Incapable, for whatever reason, of affirmative action. I was lying there on my back, stretched out like a dumb animal on a rack, naked. I tried to raise my hands to defend myself against the ferocity of her words, but there was no fighting back against the torrid heat of her breath in my face, no refusing to listen to the words that she was firing at me, like so many poisonous darts into the skin of my face, *piqures* in the night, all the terrible stinging darts of those words of hers, and many of them the same word uttered over and over, as a hammer will beat at one particular stone, again and again, until, in time, the wall, no matter how high, will begin to lean and to topple. That is how it was for me on that night. Could this be a sufficient reason to pity me?

CXLIX

As I pick apart this flower at the table, magnifying glass in hand, petal by petal, sepal by sepal, leaf by leaf, I recognise its inherent goodness. The very air seems to ring with praise this morning in its presence. I recognise the goodness of its form. I recognise the goodness of its making, so carefully constructed and with such patience, to give such boundless pleasure to the eye and the other senses. And so it will be when I too am dismembered at life's end, when I have sighed my last sigh in this village. They will pluck up the toe bone from the casket and they will say as they hover over me: see of what particles of goodness this body of his has been made. Regard the rounded smoothness of its construction. Then they will toss it from hand to hand, and perhaps even from one to another, appraising it marvellingly. Others will be busy with liver, eye or femur, inspecting them all, exchanging benign opinions. That is the nightmare of which I cannot rid myself this morning.

CL

I have asked the finger to see. I have asked the eye to feel. I have asked the nose to dig the solid ground. I have demanded a certain flexibility of this body, but it has not responded. My spirit and my body, must they forever be pulling in different directions? Must I be a servant of many masters? This morning I had a mind to fly above the rooftops – it was a cloudless day, perfect for such an enterprise – but my feet refused to budge. I cursed them for their indolence, their waywardness, their cussedness, their perversity. I stamped one upon another. I gave myself great pain. And still they were turned away from me as if busy plotting the overthrow of kingdoms wholly unknown to me.

CLI

I use the figure one in relation to myself, and yet I am not one. Surely I am several. I am forever shifting in different directions, dividing the self from the self as I go about my daily business. I am perpetually at war with myself. What is more, I am not necessarily known to myself, not entirely. How could I be, knowing myself to be so many? There is a limit, inevitably, to my own understanding of myself. There is a limit to my understanding of my several selves. Which of my several selves can be said to know me, exhaustively? Surely none of them. Each one must be invested with partial knowledge. And this is why, surely, I habitually find myself at war with my own impulses. I say to myself go, and I come. This explanation I offer to you now, here, contained within these futile words, is so partial and so clouded. It is more than enough to write down the little that I have written. I am torn apart on the rack of myself.

CLII

The voice seemed to hover at my shoulder, intimate yet disembodied, and this is what it said to me (let me record its whispered words before I begin to disbelieve myself): you have vestigial wings. My mouth yawned open in wonder. Once you flew, it surely said (although not in so many words), and now you do not. I stared down, thoroughly ashamed of myself. I had blamed my feet. I had punished them for no good reason, leaving them black and blue with bruises. And then comes this, a quite different explanation. I was consumed with dismay. I was no longer capable of doing what once I might have done. In former times I had been an angel. Now I was a man, living amongst the clodhoppers. All idle speculation? I stripped off my shirt, writhing and twisting myself out of its sleeves with more adroitness than I had shown in weeks. I began to examine my shoulder blades. I felt around with my fingers for some hint of nubbyness. I sought out a vestige of those strange, unearthly protrusions. I could feel nothing. Was it all a lie then? Who would feed me such lies? I slipped my arms back into my shirt – I was shuddering and shivering – and as I did so, I felt a great lightening of the body, as if I was as buoyant and as free as the air itself, as if I was again what that voice had once proclaimed me as having been (though not in so many words). Flinging out my painfully thin arms – and even whirling them in the air – I walked towards the door and the heady promise of a new day with a certain immeasurable confidence.

CLIII

I curse the fragments of this once so precious bowl, my old coffee bowl, sometime so fast a friend. Was it truly I who had said such words aloud to myself? I remembered the days and the days when it had served me so well, when I had filled it to the brim, and taken my first edifying sips of the morning, piping hot to the lips, and how, pushing it away a little, coquettishly, raising it a little more and even tilting it on its axis, I had always been in the habit of staring and staring into the brownness of its glaze, thinking as I did so of the hue of the goatskin pelt of John the Baptist, that rude forerunner amongst men. How I had cherished it above almost all things else! It had always kept its own prized place on that shelf, at the level of my eye, so that when I turned to the sink, as I did so often, it would always be there to greet me. And then, one morning of heavy cloud cover my fingers had been slippery with water, and I had lost it. It had crashed against the tiles of the floor and shattered into a thousand tiny, heart-rending fragments, and as I stared at it down there, that once most beloved of objects, I had said to myself: how I loathe fragments and all that they represent. Life, if it is to be anything at all, must be a Unity.

CLIV

It has gone on again, on and on, throughout the night, that singing from behind or beyond – it is never quite possible to say – the walls. Those high-piping voices. The voices of angels? The voices of cherished castrati? Strange echoings of phrase bouncing off phrase. I have tried – I have even been eager at first – to join in the chorus, but my voice, always so poor an instrument, has been incapable of climbing to so lofty a pitch. I am a prisoner on the lower slopes, stuck fast here, unable to proceed to the sunlit heights. And when I raise my eyes to the sun glare, I can see them all there, on those sunlit heights, row upon row of them, such able choristers. There is something else that troubles me: what is the language in which they are singing? It is neither Greek nor Latin. And is it in fact singing at all that I am hearing? What begins in singing often seems to modulate into squealings and squeakings and scrapings and gratings. The squeaking of the edge of a naked blade against a sink. The slow turning of rusted wheels, grinding one against another. Cog buffeting cog. Strangulated mice in their death throes. What has been heavenly quickly plunges to the level of the truly diabolical. It is then that I find myself sitting bolt upright. I stare around in wonder and near disbelief. Is everything as it once was? Yes, everything is indeed as it once was. That great hulking beast of a church sits four-square on its old familiar ground just beyond the window. It has seen me. It has known me to the core. My chair faces away from me with a measure of coldness, a measure of indifference. I take its customary habits in good part. I know its ways. Settling myself again, I rehearse snatches of wonders inside my own head – Bach, Couperin, Dupré, that holy trinity, the blessed three – before I invite sleep to engulf me.

CLV

I am riding, so easily, on the waves of the air. When I activate the muscles in my face, I recognise that I am smiling to myself. I am also winking. In short, it is evening again, balmy and mild, in all its amiable, autumnal plumpness. I raise my arm until it hovers, trembling a little, in parallel with the surface of this desk, and I then allow my pen to float away from my grip, so easily. I release it from between finger and thumb to the accompaniment of a blown kiss. O, to be done with my words! I watch with calm fascination as, much to my surprise, ink begins to stream from its tip. Thin arabesques appear in the air in front of my face, forming new words which I fail to recognise. Throtchsphohlomens, for example. They come on, they come on, so eagerly. They are so eager to be born! And there are so many of them. I interrogate them one by one, quite gently at first because they are words which have streamed from my own pen, and can therefore be said – surely – to be my words. And yet I recognise that there exists a huge and unbudgeable door between us. I can utter the music of those words, but I cannot enter into their presence. They will not admit me. They are evidently happy in the company of a stranger beyond the door, that stranger who is capable of investing them with meaning, and a stranger moreover whom I have conjured into being, or so it seems, in so far as I have invented for him a language of communication. I may therefore, in part at least, be living his life. I must therefore, in part at least, be that stranger. Which means that I must be seeing myself as through a glass darkly on this balmy autumnal evening. There is no other adequate explanation.

CLVI

Let me tell you this, in all confidence. I am in the throes of reducing my life to a series of small, severe, local rituals, one for each finely diced portion of the day. It is how I am learning to cope with my life as it rages through its crises. It is how I give it the words to speak back to me in the absence of the clamour of others. And there is no real cleansing, no genuine opening up of the self to the self, without the absence of others. And yet the word reduced is not one that seems to describe this development adequately. It demeans. It diminishes. It makes me look more puny and less otherworldly than I honestly believe myself to be. Aggrandised then? Perhaps. Perhaps not. There is no flourish of trumpets accompanying the way I have chosen to live my life. I creep forward, moment by moment, in silence. Of what then does it consist exactly? What are these small acts of ritual? The first and the greatest and the least conspicuous to the outside world would surely be the opening – the ungumming – of the left eye immediately after waking. How to ensure that it admits the dawn light with extreme slowness, as if receiving through the netting of a kitchen sieve the most profound of miracles. And this is the truth, of course. The day's new light is surely the greatest of all miracles. We move, so swiftly, from darkness to darkness. There is scant time, and much of that is so impoverished, in between. Eternity lies in wait at either end. The temptation, always, is to bound forward like a dog eager for its morning food, its prolonged act of urination, back leg raised as if in mock-salute. I hold myself back therefore when I become aware of myself rising to consciousness. I take a grip on myself. I breathe the one word that will surely rein me in: hallowed.

CLVII

Learn this from me. Daily, I am beginning to make so much of so little. More and more, in fact. I look at each word that I lay down on this sheet. I pull it apart. I dismember it. I see into its interstices for shades of light and darkness, ever finer degrees of thickness and thinness. I take advantage of the habits of the ant, the fly, the cockroach, the beetle. Their busyness. Their steady, regular application. Their unstoppability. They make so much of so little. I strive to humble myself, to live within a narrower and ever narrower compass. And I thereby enrich the least little thing. I suck longer on a stale crust of bread, for example. I seek out its hidden riches. I divide each crust into two equal halves, and I batten down on each half with my gums, softening it, savouring it, sucking on it, gently pulling at it, for a similar length of time. I admire the grace of the grass blade. I run my nail down its crease. I admire its symmetry. I put it to my lips and, squeezing it between my two thumbs, I make it squeal like a being at the mercy of a torturer. I take extreme pleasure, when humming to myself, to hold the exact same note – low, medium or high – for moments on end. What begins in monotony ends in beatitude, that is my daily discovery. I am learning to raise up the dirt in my fingernails. I am learning to savour the sweetness of the dirt. Am I alone to be despised?

CLVIII

The very last word to be said. The gravest of grave matters then. What such a word might be, plucked from the millions at one's disposal, which swarm in the upper air like the pesky midges of high summer. The loved and the unloved, all in violent contention. Not any word though. Not a matter of relative indifference. My word for a start. Not his. Not hers. Not some other's. Finished. Finished? And yet the word itself is not a perfect conclusion. It is the announcement of a conclusion, the prolegomenon to a conclusion. What is more, it is deliciously, savoursomely bi-syllabic. It hangs over itself, self-admiringly, self-preeningly. It seems to announce to the hearer: attend to me in all my heart-stopping sonority. It has an appetite to linger and make ample space for itself. It demands attention. It requires to be looked at. It is not asking to be dismissed lightly. It is in fact craving to be praised for the fact that it is perfectly apposite. A much shorter word then, a word starkly, swiftly conclusive, curtly self-dismissive, and almost self-loathing. Not? Perhaps not. Yes, not.

CLIX

I am not exaggerating. I am not stretching my words. You have a duty to take me seriously. Let me say it again in order to convince you. All this that surrounds me here in this house, I have created it with my own unerring eye. I have conjured it from almost nothing. Without my seeing, it would indeed be nothing. Yet this also is true and undeniable: it is almost nothing. It teeters on the brink of the uttermost insignificance. No other eye but mine would take it for a rarity, if not a miracle. They would mutter these words to themselves and then they would pass on, so eager to be away: table, chair, window, steep-rising staircase, teetering ziggurat of mouldering antique books. They would regard this world of mine, in its entirety, as perfectly humdrum, and perhaps even to be pitied or despised, because they do not have the capacity to see into it. They do not know – how could they know? – what I make of these things. They have never witnessed how I have constructed my life from them. They see only my dull and infinitely repeatable regularities, my numbing simplicities, the witlessness of my everyday journeyings from here to there – from the raising up of a leg to the setting down of a leg – and then back again. They do not understand how I have lifted each thing up, one by one, and set it apart. They do not guess – how could they? – that I have sanctified my life by the way that I have chosen to live it. They know me only as slope-shouldered, taciturn and impassive, with all the elegance of a rusting hulk of machinery abandoned at the corner of a field. The field behind this house perhaps.

CLX

I am always catching myself on the brink of an exclamation. Words to clear the air. Words to bless the world again with a new and perfect roundedness. Words to drive away these louring clouds which hang over me like a curse from an undisclosed source of tunnelling malevolence. It begins in a vague aura of excitement, the surprising jolt of a pulsing in the veins of the left wrist, a catching sight of a something wholly admirable just beyond the window: the helter-skelter skittering of a rabbit, for example, going in no particular direction, driven on by a kind of glorious, stinging madness, or by the fact of its own running to nowhere in particular – or so it seems. At sights such as these, a door seems to spring open inside myself, and my life, once again, proclaims itself, with a great inner cry, to be boundless. I am in the grip of everything that I might ever be. There is no one standing, stern-faced, to the left or the right of me to say: no, that is not to be. I run and I run, and there is no stopping me.

CLXI

I have craved to snatch some pauses, a breathing space or two, between the various scenes of my life, but it is quite impossible, I see that now. There is nothing but the slow ticking of this steady continuity, the gradual shift from youthfulness to decrepitude. There is no flitting back and forth. The wheels must keep on turning. I have yearned to take drastic action, to drain myself of my life's blood for a day or to interrupt the onward beating of the heart for just as long as it might take to make a new beginning. A false assumption. To stop the heart is to make an end of it all, to say: *finis.* There is to be no new beginning for me, that is now perfectly evident. Everything must attach to everything else like children who dance in a ring, moments linking hands with moments. Everything must continue on its accustomed way, dull-wittedly. If death could be simulated for a moment, that would be a new beginning. But death comes once, and it is not to be returned from.

<h3 style="text-align: center;">CLXII</h3>

A fly calls to me, wheedlingly, maddeningly. It encircles my head. It swoops towards my ear, and then quickly veers away, in order to give me time to formulate my fly ruminations. Returning, it quickly poses an entire syllabus of fly-questions. I flick it away. I give it no space, no respect, no time, no affection. It sits on the edge of the table, biding its time. It wrings its hands as I write, and when I am almost finished, it lands on the back of my hand. It watches how my pen is poised. It needs the reassurance that the last word I write today will be an acknowledgement of the importance of its presence in my life, and so, with the utmost care, I raise my pen and I write it into my life: fly.

<h3 style="text-align: center;">CLXIII</h3>

Or so they said. I did not hear the words myself. I was absent on that day. I was going about my daily business. They were passed to another, who duly passed them on to me. Swiftly, courteously. Words of plain dealing. Words of stark reasonableness. Words of the utmost clarity. And yet when I came to read them, the words had gone. The sheet was white as snow. They had been there once, I knew that for a fact, because the paper was still warm to the touch. In fact, it burned my finger ends slightly. And yet those words of uplift, admonition, correction, exhortation had been removed from my sight. And so now it has become my task and my burden to inscribe my own words over those words, and on that very same sheet of paper. Words of the utmost clarity. Words of admonition. Words of correction. Words of exhortation. And when the page is full to brimming over, I paste them to my brow for all to see. It is my own particular branding. Now I am seared forever.

CLXIV

I am drawing everything to a stop. I am drawing everything to a close on these long, cold winter mornings of slow experimentation. This is how things are to be, how I am to comprehend the scope of myself: there must be a tinkering or a meddling with that self until it yields up its treasures; a drawing to the surface of its most hidden reserves. I have discovered this: the intellect is at its most productive when the body is at its most inert, when it is utterly immobile, trapped, slumped deep and wholly flaccid in this chair, within reach of the sun's eye, my sole interlocutor. All this is good. In fact, it could not be better, when the body has nowhere to go, no urge to remove itself elsewhere, and there are none of the distractions associated with movement of any kind, from the slow, small and lacklustre to the feverish. At such moments I am enabled – I enable myself – to contemplate nothing but the movements of my own thought. It is a question of purification. And yet, and yet...how then to record these gifts of the intellect, how to remember if the pen is condemned to be utterly immobile? Memory is so utterly undependable. What is more, it is mendacious.

CLXV

There is a certain ill defined physical pain or bodily unease which I associate with that day of the week, and by that I mean her day. Yes, I feel how it is, so strongly, when she leaves me again. The house feels it too, and I am profoundly in touch – how could this not be the case? – with the spirit of this house. We are as one in regretting her departure. And yet what does she do exactly other than cook, clean, sit, and sew when I ask her to sew? She does not speak – I would not encourage speech. She does not look, except at the floor and, occasionally, to the accompaniment of a small sigh, beyond the window, as if to say: that is where I belong. Which is all to the good in the scheme of things. I would not encourage the exchange of looks between us. All she does is to slither her feet from place to place, doing that which is physically necessary to crockery, chair, table, sweeping up the dust of the week from the floor in her metal pan – how it scrapes across the floor! – and then standing over, head bowed, as if in prayerful silence, and letting it slip deep into her bucket, which she then removes from the kitchen with a single high swing, and places on the doorstep. She displaces the air, perhaps. Is that of significance to me, that she fans the air with her bustly movements, leaving behind her very particular bodily odours, which are not necessarily wholly unpleasant? I have a mind to go after them when she has left me. I have a mind to trap them in a box, except that such a thing is not exactly compatible with clarity of mind or sweet reasonableness. What is more, I would have no way to prevent their escape.

CLXVI

I am surprised that I have not spoken of it until this moment: the sound of prayer rising up into the air, that wild rocketing goodness knows whither. Its efficacy. Its inner dynamics. The speeding of a certain ill-defined yearning. Can all that really be true? It was once true. It had a certain quality of special pleading. Or is it this only: a voice muttering thinly into the void? Is that what in the end it must come down to? Do I even cherish the sound of my own voice? And am I really praying when I am merely speaking out loud to myself of the things of the day? Am I enriched and reassured by the sound of my own voice? Perhaps this voice gives succour and comfort because it is no longer quite my own voice when I speak. When I open my mouth, when I expel such shapes of sound, they not only drift away from me, they also seem to take on the very characters of the voices of the few that I have known and cherished in my life. They choose the very words that I have spoken to make themselves known to me, to make their presences felt anew within me. I can even see them walking towards me. Some go as if to sit down beside me, pointing to the bed's edge or to a place near my feet on the floor - such is their desperation, it seems - but I am too particular to allow them to linger.

CLXVII

My greatest burden is this: the fear of endlessness. To be rehearsing the same thoughts, the same verbal formulations, again and again. To stare into the glass, and to see the same face again, a touch more wizened and helpless and dispensable.

CLXVIII

I hear them as I go about my daily business, words, words, words, issuing from mouths in a disconnected series of random ejaculations. Volleys, as if from a hunter's gun down in the valley. They assail my inner ear. They bruise me. I catch at them, one by one, in a vain attempt to make something of them. I am always so eager to be building. Here they are then, for your interest, a small choice from these many randomnesses, heard out in the street this morning. *Such as that day. Fatter than any pig. He came and then he went again. She pushed and then she pushed. Could it have been him, really?* Is that enough? Have I convinced you? I take them back to my laboratory in the house, by which I mean this table top, this notebook. And then I endeavour to make something of them, these random scatterings, remnants of lives which are flying off at all times in all directions. Why are they always so unruly? Some of them are my words, of course. They are the words that are on my tongue's tip, day and night. I greet them with warmth and affection. And yet they are also not my words because they have issued from another's mouth. They merely sound the same. And they have such threatening neighbours. I am always so careful to choose amiable neighbours for each word in my vocabulary. When words go astray, when words fall into the wrong company, insurrection is in the offing.

CLXIX

Here then is the problem. I can be said to know myself only in so far as I am able to say: this is the I which I interrogate every morning. This is the eye which I greet on waking. Then the doubts begin to assail me with such words as these. Wrong. You do not know yourself, not at all, because what is known of you is random, imperfect, and composed of parts, inclinations, passing whimsies, which appear to skitter away from each other even as you go to capture them within the intense and narrow compass of this beam of light which you describe so proudly as the life of the mind... It must also be said that a certain arrogance goes hand in hand with this so called knowledge of myself that I am said to possess, a certain reckless striking out in the direction of unwavering certainty. I arrive at my own finger post in the village, pointing, unswervingly, in the direction of myself. I stand there, admiringly. Surely that is proof enough that I have staked myself out, that I have mapped my own kingdom. Mapping itself is certain proof of the existence of that kingdom.

CLXX

It is my task, always, to interrogate this silence, to know it for what it is, to feel the reassurance of its ever thickening darkness, to sound its depths, to live within its secure impenetrabilities. In short, silence is the ultimate perfection. That is why we so much crave to live within its untroubled borders. Everything that is not silence is noisome distraction, and no one of sound mind would surely wish to be distracted, to have the head jerked to left or right by random flashings of light, brayings of sound. Silence is a temple within which to live, and the self becomes its own temple the longer it lives within the ever rising walls of silence. First you suffer impatience. You crave the fullness of the world. You want the self to be scattered abroad. You yearn to live the life of a chameleon.

And then, little by little, a modicum of calmness begins to descend. You learn peace, steadfastness and quietude. You discover that there is nothing to be learned, nothing to be known, which is greater than this. This is the height and the depth of it all. This is your own fullness, your beginning and your end, a fitting and final conclusion to the body's restlessness.

CLXXI

Every day, the ceaseless endeavour to reach a conclusion of sorts, to summarise, to tidy away so that the caterwauling creature falls dumb. This set apartness or self-estrangement, as a form of security, specious self-betterment. No better world than this one, comes the whisper, of unassailable and unreachable loneliness. One from another. Bone from bone. Flesh from flesh. The yawning gulf between hand clasp and hand clasp, mouth and mouth, body and body. The holding of the self upright, as if challenging the world to do its worst. And the letting it fall to the bed again, stripped bare, unregarded, unloved, as so much detritus. The question again, the ever repeated question: can this be all? The answer, as ever: this is all. There is no more than this. Look in vain for more than this. The steely, steady apportionment of blame, always so vexatious in its inevitability. The structures we have created – how tall they seem to rise into the sky! – to tame our animal natures. And then the tearing down of such structures at moments of war, revolution. The greatest of these being the puffed up self. And the turning one's back on that self in self-disgust. Appeals to infinity. Appeals to the god within and without us. Where to find him. Whither he fled and when exactly. The need to continue and then continue until the foot stumbles and head hits concrete, conclusively. The outcome: dust blown on the wind.

CLXXII

No stopping this crying out. The mouth will not close. The mouth refuses to obey. The mouth will not take no for an answer. Particular shapes of crying out when seen in the air: the circular, as in a great, tunnelling wind-blast of torment. And then, the tiniest of complaints, as if the smallest of horizontal slits in the door to admit the thinnest of letters: wheedling, when so little is being made of so little.

CLXXIII

This is how I remember it. It is how I shall always remember it. I was caught up by the wind that morning, lifted up above the house, and I found myself drifting ocean-ward, towards the west. The chilliness of the wind in those upper regions of the air had no adverse effect upon me whatsoever. I even found myself smiling as I fanned my arms. To be shifting westwards like this, so steadily, was a kind of relaxation. When I looked down, I saw Paul walking below me, miles below me. He had passed through the graveyard, and now he was approaching the house, head bowed. There was nothing other than this sight of him, walking. All else had been erased. It was unmistakably Paul, walking, with a ferocious onward purposiveness. All that customary serenity had been wiped from his face. Instead, there was anger, anger, anger. He had been staring at my desk beside the window. He had expected me to be sitting there, recollecting him, paying him my customary homage. Instead I had flittered away, quite lightly, quite carelessly, like a sheet of blank paper lifted by the wind. He needed me. He wanted me. That was the greatest part of it, that he wanted me, such as I was, such as I am, such as I will always be. With all my forward creepings.

CLXXIV

The rest of it continues around me – I see it all there, fanning out before me; it ravishes the eye – like a kind of theatre of impromptu happenings, prompted into existence for no particular reason. Or perhaps it is a whirligig, forever flying and turning and outflinging. Yes, call it a kind of theatre at which I am forever present, appraising each gesture – arm thrown out, leg raised at a ridiculous angle, grimace, cry. I enumerate all the customary themes: a death in the family, the incarceration of the snivelling, shifty-eyed criminal, the swift slitting of some pig's throat behind the barn. All this numbing dailyness intrigues me, how no one baulks at it, no one rages, no one protests. It always continues, with such dedication, as if these are lives being lived with a purpose. Not so. Not at all. They are words fallen out of a mouth at random, an anyhow rock slide down the side of a mountain. I sit through it all with such rigidity. I go about my business of categorisation. I am nothing but this observing eye. I do not participate in any of the rest. I speak, I gesticulate as little as possible. I am utterly outside it all.

CLXXV

Water. My water content. My content is water. My contentment is water. There is nothing else to be had. It is my all in all. I am buoying myself up. The slop and the heave of me. The flesh dissolving back into water, as if by way of an apology for itself. The words losing their shapes, slow-collapsing into the meaningless dribble of unreadable formlessness. The body, once so present and so opposed, becoming nothing other than a fading splash across these boards across which I pace, back and forth, again and again, a black, vanishing, contourless map of sorts. When they enter to make my acquaintance, to suck of my usefulness in matters of the soul, I am gone. I have conveniently removed myself by evaporating into the empty air just moments before their arrival. I have dried away to nothingness. When I close my eyes, I see water rising and rising until all else is wholly occluded. It is good to be water, on this or any other day, accountable to no one, no longer rebarbative stuff or prickly flesh, no longer opinionated. What is more, you want for no one and nothing, being water. You are also useful. You want me now and forever, do you not, for being the water that I am. You raise me up – if you can catch me at all – and you drink me down. A long, health-giving draught, to the accompaniment of long sighs of pleasure. You cannot but welcome me. Until, that is, there arrives that ominous day on which I choose to add a pinch of strychnine to myself because you are paying me so little regard. I have become mere water to you.

<h2 style="text-align:center">CLXXVI</h2>

I have understood nothing. The walnut tree in this garden, so sage-like in its ancient, strangulating gnarledness, is wholly inscrutable to me, as is the stem of this hollyhock, once beside the back gate, which I have just snapped off and laid across the threshold of the house, on the topmost step, as if it were an omen of sorts. No matter what the attention I give it – whether I lay it down or twirl it in the air like a baton of sorts – I can still make nothing of it. It gives nothing back to me. And even if I were to understand its physical properties, to locate it precisely within its family, give it a meaningful grounding in quite particular terminology, it would still give nothing back to me. It would still look back at me blankly, whistling quite brazenly, with such maddening insouciance, its stranger's song. And this is how the world grows upon me now, day by day, like a mould of sorts. It thins out. Little by little it fades and retreats from me. And consequently I find that I need fewer and ever fewer words with which to describe it because words, once so rich and so connected to the things of the eye – how the eye was once glutted by the things of this world! – they too are withdrawing

from me. They too seem to look increasingly self-conscious when I lift them up for careful appraisal – which happens, it has to be said, less and less. They too seem to blame me for all this woeful shrinkage. Am I to be blamed then? Or are you, in so far as you never respond to my words?

CLXXVII

The music goes around and about, a riddling drone. I wait, hands clasped, counting the thinning ranks of the faithful, the ever fewer. I have raised myself above them in this place. This is where I am condemned to be rooted. It has been my life-long mission, my duty, my reason for being. I have put on this mask of solemnity, such awkward solemnity. They look in my direction, though often not directly. Some catch my eye. Others observe the circling movement of a fly or the slow sifting of dust motes down through the air. Yet another attends to a child, barely visible to my eye, who pouts and squirms to be away. Who in his heart of hearts would not prefer to taste the freshness of the air on this May morning, to sip at a cooling breeze beyond these walls, these windows? Voices rise and swell or fall away in unison, to the accompaniment of the many familiar piping tunes, tunes which haunt the memory, some grave, others wincingly sentimental. I stand above them here, puppet-like, raised up inside this machinery of wood, two arms raised and spread in a welcome of sorts. My mouth is open. It is speaking words, customary words, words of reassurance, words of comfort, words that will ever be returning, week in, week out, words which cause us to rise up inside ourselves, but also to cower and to fear a little. Must we not forever be falling short of what these words expect from us? And all these are borrowed words, solemnly bequeathed to us by the dead, and repeated over and over. And I listen to myself saying them, over and over. A vision, momentary, seizes hold of me. I see some of them, trapped up there between the rafters like bats. Bat-like they flutter about our

heads. Those bats have surely fallen from my mouth. And there is no alternative to any of this. This is how it must always be until I am carried from this place and another voice speaks these self-same words in my stead. It will be the same voice, though it will not be my voice. Not exactly my voice, though haunted by my voice, just as I myself have been haunted by those other voices.

CLXXVIII

When they come, the words are very simple, and almost inevitable. Why did you ask me? I did not ask you. You came of your own accord. You had your eyes on the ground. You were looking for the path. It was as if a gentle wind had carried you in my direction. I scarcely noticed that it was happening. The days, months, years of my life had been so ordinary. I had gone from growing child to bewildered youth in the blink of an eye and nothing had impeded me. That is how so often it begins, in bewilderment, which is a kind of unfathomable haunting. Then all this bewilderment, little by little, falls away as I begin to see you, ahead of me, gently beckoning. The truth is that I did not know you for who or what you were. I regarded you as one stranger amongst many. My life had been a huddle of strangers until that moment. You were nothing unusual. That is the way of things. Nothing is made clear until the final moment, the moment of revelation. You speak of it as something infinitely precious, and to be desired above all things else. Is this not how it has been for you? Let me stop you there. You are speaking untruths. I am drifting. I do not even know who is whispering these words into my ear as I sleep.

CLXXIX

The path is infinite in extent and extremely narrow, barely broader than the width of my foot, which is why I can never set one foot beside another. I inch along it, second by anguished second, with such fear, such hesitation. My balance has not been good for many years, and now, needless to say, it is much worse. Were I a tightrope walker, I would be gripping a horizontal pole, which would be steadying me. My stunted arms, flung out and forever trembling, must suffice me. I have walked so short a distance. If I were to dare to turn and look back, I would see where I once began, at that tiny square of scorched ground beside which I used to sit. It is in that far corner of the garden, which used to catch the morning sun. That was a place I once loved to love. I have been moving along now for years – or so it seems – and I have managed a metre or two at best, and I have no idea when or where or whether it will ever end. My fear is of falling because this path is raised up so high above the earth, so high that I dare not look down for fear of plunging, down, down, down. I put one foot, with great care, in front of another, inching along minute by minute. I stare down at each succeeding foot, urging it on. I try not to stare past it. I try not to raise my face to the stars. I try not to see far in any direction whatsoever because then I would find myself in the grip of hopelessness and helplessness. There is no alternative to any of this. There is no going back. There is no one to call to. I must keep on going.

CLXXX

Blood. Skin. Nails. Bones (various). Together, needless to say, with all those sloppy, heaving, unreachable inner entanglements with which the fingers meddle at their peril. All told, it does not amount to much. It is no reason for indulging in outbursts of inordinate pride. And yet there are those who trumpet and preen and strut and caper and guffaw and roister, day and night. Which is yet another good reason to stay still in this corner, treasuring one's smallness.

CLXXXI

You were never mine, and I was never yours. From the start it has been like this. As I approached you across the kitchen floor, you receded from me, with the utmost care. You melted back into the window. And when I reached that window, you were nothing but a smudging of grey cloud above a field, tattering away to nothingness even as I raised my vaguely waving arm and spoke to you. What exactly did I say? Or did I sing? When I held you to me – sometimes I would rush towards you, and hold you to me in order to furnish myself with unassailable proof that you really existed for me in this world – I found that I was clasping to myself a smooth and ever rising column of stone, which would rise, much later, to the finically pleasing detail of a decorative capital that the connoisseur buried deep inside me would feel easily inclined to appraise. Otherwise, there was nothing. No one and nothing. And all those spaces in between. I had drawn a pack of blanknesses. Which is why I have always gone about my daily business of generating heat from within because I could trust no one and nothing to do it for me beyond the threshold of this body. I would beat my arms to my sides. I would blow on my hands. I would even shout out loud. Did that help at all? Were you beyond the door just then, attentively listening, or was it a shadow that I was seeing, another mode of trickery? You would never tell me.

CLXXXII

If this is how it is to be, then so be it. If this is how it is to be, then so be it. Can I – can you – bear so much repetition, so much tramping on to nowhere? And how can this not be the case? Otherwise, I would be tottering backwards, arms flailing, into some ridiculous dream of me. What is more, how can I even ask myself such a question when it has always been like this? And yet, and yet...some part of me rises up every morning, as if eager to begin a new kind of race, whose rules will be known only in the fullness of time. That knowledge – just that chink of forward knowledge – quickly stirs something within me. Although in body I am as slow and as aged as ever, the pulse quickens a little and the spirit sheds years of drabness and numbing repetition. I walk out into the garden, taking in the air, and if it is spring out there, I begin to summon, fingers snapping, every grass blade. I stand, palms spread homiletically, and speak to them in their thousands. They look up at me, eager-eyed, thirsting for a little water of life, ever ready to heed my call. Or, if it happens to be winter, I carry a handful of snow up to my mouth and kiss it with my lips. Guzzling at it, I numb my lips.

CLXXXIII

Here is the truth at last. It has to come down to this in the end, and this is surely the end of it all. There can be no end beyond this one, no matter that Dame Theology may rise up and, beating down with the hoof of her hand on the edge of the pulpit, speak against me. The house is broken. This old house of mine is broken. It has shed all that steady pomposity of old. It has rid itself of its outer garments. Its pediment is clean snapped in two like a biscuit – did I not see that happen with my own eyes? – and now it is quietly weeping over its own fate like some sad widow ripe for a moment's consolation. And no one but I am to blame for this. I have let the future happen. I have steadfastly turned my face against the fact of it for so many years, and now it is indubitable. The future, harsh though this may sound, has me by the throat. The wind is whipping up the stairs. Day and night it comes after me, circling the bed, round and round it goes, like a pack of hounds frothing at the muzzle, and then descending the stairs again with an almighty clickety clattering of extended claws. My every garment is too thin for my needs. Who ever paid attention to my needs? There is nowhere for me to hide. I am always too much here, in the eye of it. I am reduced to a pathetic shivering tangle of ancient bones. I would serve myself much better if I were to be heaped up in a pile and arranged (by the hunters perhaps, between their morning quaffs of pastis) in some rude sealed box behind the sanctuary as if I were some new-come saint's relic. I can hold off the packs of assailants no longer. They are stripping me of my roof. I can hear all that tearing and rending. It seems to tear and rend at my ears, my throat. My hair is thick with falling dust. I am choking on it. And now they are even tugging at the boards beneath my feet, making me do this ridiculous, hours'-long dance in order to stay upright. I have called for succour, and, hours later, I have found myself still listening to the after-echoes of my special pleading. I have called for Marie – surely it is her day again. I have seen her at last. Has she heeded my call? Is it Marie that I see taking the axe to my apple tree, or stuffing her throat with the sweetest of my quinces? It is in the likeness of Marie, certainly. And is that a *sanglier* tearing at my roots?

CLXXXIV

Parables. Parables. He heaves them by the sackful to this gate, carrying them across his back. I go out to greet him, disbelieving, bowed of head. They sit at my feet, the seven sacks, lumpish and squirming. He has dumped them there for my edification. I open to see a thorn tree, rising from stony ground. I am the spike at its end. I have been reduced to a spike of sheer malevolence. So be it, Lord. I sit there in wait, in those parched desert lands, wholly indifferent to the passage of time. I wait and I wait. I see a puff of dust approaching from the distance. It is a man. A finger rises to touch me. It is my neighbour's finger. I reach out to greet it. I make it bleed. I watch the blood oozing. He howls with pain as he hops away. I sun myself for days on end, patiently waiting, always unknowing, fiercely attentive and yet unknowing. How can that be? Then I fade into darkness. I have done with myself. Next I am a young seed, broadcast by His hand. I watch myself flying through the air, the smoothness of my curve as I fall. I see myself entering a tiny hole in the ground. For months I lie there, in the dark. I clench my teeth in the darkness, wondering how long, how long. I wail, but my wailing - it almost deafens me - does not spread beyond the outer limits of myself. Will something happen? I say to myself. Will nothing happen? Then, little by little, I feel myself beginning to rise and to rise - it is as if I am awakening from a long sleep - until I am a handsome and mature fig tree. I savour the plumpness of my own fruit. And then one day He walks past me with a gaggle of eager listeners. He swipes at me with his stick in passing - he is not even paying much attention to me. I fall to the ground, wholly disbelieving. Everything must begin again.

CLXXXV

It was as much as we always had in those days. And it was so very little. The tiniest stain on a finger's end. A blushing. A hint. The merest suggestion. Whose though? And, if so, why hers? No matter. Taste it then. Taste its sweetness. Taste its acridity. Do it. One or another. Sometimes we would choose not to taste at all. We would decide to savour, as evidence of the encouragement that was being offered to our growing lives, the very fact that we were being given the wherewithal to make something of ourselves. That we were, after all, deserving. That someone was reaching out to us. That there was not after all one and then another, and all wholly indifferent to each other. That, as a chorus or a community, we could all bend over this tiny, precious specimen of nourishment, caught, suspended, within this tiny glass phial, and recognise it for what it was. We could then rise up and give thanks. We could even raise it up above our heads and process - as on some saint's day around the perimeter of the *potager* - and then sing, all day, toe to toe, on the grass, quite forgetting the smallness of it, quite forgetting that it was all that had been bequeathed to us, on that day or any other.

CLXXXVI

You have been here before. You made this earth, this place, and everything that surrounds it. You know the ground on which I stand. You dug this ground. You stamped it down to make it stable. You created this space for me. You slotted me into it with finicky attention. You have also questioned me and measured me. You have approved of me. You have nodded me through. Had all this not happened, all this preliminary work on our – our? – behalf, I would surely not be here at all. There would be no idle talk of me in this neighbourhood. Had I not been regarded as true, worthy or viable in some sense, I would not wake up as I do, expecting to be alive, expecting to face forward as I do. I would not be throwing back the shutters and blinking into the light. I would not have the will to avoid your eye. I would not have the wherewithal to say to you, minute by minute or second by second (it entirely depends upon my mood): do not approach too close. You promised to let me live my own life.

CLXXXVII

Whether this book is dead or not is a serious matter. A matter not to be considered before sleep or there will be no sleep. There will be an endless staring into the dark. Every morning that I suffer from the miracle of new-waking, I see it there again, waiting for me, seemingly harmless as ever, black and mute and self-contained, on the outer edge of the table top, almost at the limits of itself. That is its customary position, at the outer limits. It is, in short, a book of extremities, and it exists out there on the cold outer extremities, where the serious things are done and said. Where there is no gainsaying. This book has no truck with frivolity. Its words adhere to you. There is no rubbing them away. Although it consists of mere words, you cannot rid yourself of those words. Nor, finally, would you wish to do so. Who would wish to be regarded as a feather blown on the wind? This book roots you. It ties you down. It tethers you to your own destiny. It also reveals you to be paper-thin. At such times you might wish to remonstrate with it. You might go to throw it down. It will not be thrown down. It will not be harmed or destroyed. It will always rise up again. Its words will always be present to you, materially, immaterially.

<h1 style="text-align:center">CLXXXVIII</h1>

'la distance désespérée nous laisse le temps de mourir...'

Death is not, however, on the agenda. There are those solitary islands, of course – bony, rocky, distant, treeless spaces – where I have walked, infrequently. I have sniffed at the cooling breezes. I have said to myself, Paul, poeticising rashly: enchanted islands, islands more beautiful than my forgetfulness. *Iles plus belles que l'oubli.* Thank you. I have even greeted one or two, in passing. No more than that. And then I have also said to myself, quite forthrightly: death is not on the agenda, not yet at least. You must understand that. I have said it to myself quite sternly. Remember your place in this world. You must not become a disgrace to yourself and others. And then I have looked at myself in the glass. I have turned my head side on in order to scrutinise the thinness and the nervy tightness (perhaps) of the profile. I have noted down later how I have been gradually withdrawing from myself, step by lingering step, moment by halting, breathy moment, walking behind myself in the street, barely attending to the words that I use. And then, little by little, I have come to. I have watched myself coming to, as if rising from the deeps. I have thrown back my head and laughed at myself. I have seized hold of my head and yanked it upright.

CLXXXIX

.... Is this right?

CXC

Someone then said to me, rudely interrupting my thinking: go to the West, my friend. The air is better in those parts. You will surely find yourself there. But I had already lost track of myself. When I turned, and then turned again, I would not be quite sure, having finally come to rest, somewhat dizzy, in which direction I was facing. Is there no sun riding high in the sky then? someone would say to me. But would I, being I, ever listen? No, I would not. They do say though that the West is a cool and refreshing place to be. And that has always been my habit, to be of a cool and refreshing disposition, sliding across the surface of this life of mine, and not so easily bedding down. Except in this house, of course, where I bed me down with the utmost assurance. Why so? Because I know its every inch. I have close scrutinised its every darkest crack and cranny. There is no part of it which is not intimately known to me, and which does not contain a little of me, whether it be the fragment of a finger nail or a modicum of fresh spilled blood from goodness knows where. Nose blood? Ear blood? Finger blood? Yes, I do recognise especially my own stains of blood, no matter how small and randomly strewn. What is more, they are of huge significance to me, as if they might belong, rather alarmingly, to some other. And yet when I get down on my hands and knees and sniff the boards, taking in the rich and heady aroma of it all, I know them quite unmistakably to be my own and no one else's.

CXCI

Turn in this way, he suggested, pointing to the bench of wood. It sat in the corner of the garden, slotted in so neatly there, looking so solid and dependable. There was a certain pleasing symmetry everywhere. Everything was fresh watered, gleaming, and of the brightest green. Almost platitudinous. Let us begin then, he added. Added to what though? I did not ask. He was already seated beside me, eyes drilling, pencil raised above his blank sheet of paper. There were others overlooking in that place, many of them, but they made no noise, and I paid them no heed. Truth to tell, I was wholly collected on that day – like a nut inside its tight and weathered kernel. I had wholly prepared myself. Then there began the questioning, after which we exchanged many pleasantries about foodstuffs and various bodily motions. The questions had slipped by so easily – like a young woman skipping across some sun-struck meadow. I had barely seemed to notice them coming and going, such had been the ease with which I responded. It was almost as if I had been gifted with the answers. But when we then turned to more intimate matters, the lobes of my brain seemed to darken and to tighten. I watched my hands rising up to my face. I watched with no small degree of embarrassment as they clutched at my cheeks. I had become like a small child again.

CXCII

Can there ever have been such a night of my life? And it has to be said that I have lived so many lives, and all so neatly contained within the one life. Wholly extended, like an over-strung string. Not an inch further, in any direction. The ceiling, that dark interrogator, pressing down upon me. My chair rocking and listing, as if at sea. To remain wholly still at such times, that is the challenge. The dribblings, the droolings, the inner quakings will all stop. Her face will remove itself, back to that letter in which she still refers to herself as my only friend, my only mother. I do not own that letter any more. It does not own any part of me. I remember how I held it out once in the garden, between thumb and finger, distastefully, waiting for the wind to carry it away, the thundering hail stones to spit down upon it, rending and shredding it to the smallest of rags and tatters, which I could then mash and grind into the gravel with my heel.

CXCIII

It is as if this day is waiting for the next day, in no particular hurry. All is hushed and mysteriously orderly. All is lying in wait, and so undemonstratively. I prepare myself, needlessly, for what is to come, deploying once again my range of hand gestures across the sink, pushing my fond objects around the surface of the kitchen table, rehearsing all my familiar tunes. It is all so needless, this fond urge to participate. The future is always making its own secretive preparations in my stead. There is no need for me to intervene at all. I could stand here, laughable ghost that I am, stock still, fully clothed, for eight or more hours together if I so chose, eyes closed, having driven all vain thoughts from my head, and still it would come on again in the fullness of time, gently surging ahead, that familiar, small seepage of light beneath the door, and then I would step up and open the door, and all would be ready. Tomorrow would have arrived. I ask no gesture of pardon for my fanciful habits. I weigh my own measure of indifference to all of this. I still find it wanting.

CXCIV

If I were to step up boldly for once and ask of whomever all that there is to be known, interrogate the hollyhocks or this sprig of pungent lavender which I am rolling so expertly between thumb and finger... The answer, surely, is this: the coming answer will be

my answer alone, not some other's, because all is sifted through the self which interrogates the silence of the world. There is no other voice but my voice. And it feels Other to me, surely, because I am so unfamiliar to myself. The doubts then begin to intensify. I continue to rehearse the same repertoire of questions. I do it because this voice is so strange to me that it must be the voice of that dependable stranger who is standing in front of me now to give me succour. And yet these are my own eyes into which I am staring, and this is the surface of my own mirror.

CXCV

There are certain bruisings and clottings, of the will or of the body. Do I make myself clear? The consequence is that they throw a certain screen or screens in front of me when I walk, haltingly, in any particular direction, and there are so many ways to be erring. I do not exactly know any longer in which way I am going, who has decided and why, on that day, that hour. It merely happens, and I seem to follow, sheepish, unhurried. The screens themselves – let me pause a moment to describe them – are rich, velvety, heavy on the shoulder blades when they weigh across me, bowing me forward as if I am scarcely capable of sustaining the weight and perhaps even the majestic authority of them. They envelop me wholly. I cannot see through them. Can I see into them? Is it not in fact true that when I look into them, I seem to be sipping at nigh unimaginable distances, and it is all there, in potential, all at once, so wide ranging and so free, the whole of my life, yet in no particular order, flowing ahead of me, and still beckoning me on to some exhilarating somewhere or nowhere of a place? Or perhaps these are places, several, many, and each one is so different and so special. Where I will be offered all those manifold delights which are as yet unknown to me. Let me savour this screen then, one or more of them. Let me savour them for their fruitfulness, their enveloping warmth, their many curious consolations.

CXCVI

You asked me for an invitation. You made the suggestion quite deliberately, barely whispering the words, and I felt inclined to acknowledge you as you stood there just beyond my gate, with the mist rising behind you. You were a small, timid supplicant of my favours, and my heart went out to you. I had questions to ask of you, many, and they began to rise in my throat as I looked at you. They were all preparing themselves to be spoken. But your small mouth was already closed now, and I could tell from your fixed, earnest, downward gaze that you did not wish to be questioned in this way. You yourself were the questioner. That is what your earnest gaze had made clear to me. And so I lifted you, very quietly, and with the utmost care, and carried you, side on, as if you were a beam belonging to a roof, a missing beam, up the steps, through the door, and into the kitchen, being very careful not to bruise you. You protested not at all. You seemed to expect that this was the way you would be treated. At first I laid you across several chairs, and then I found a box in which to place you, a comfortable dwelling all would surely agree, with mouth hole, arm holes and space for your legs to show some curiosity. And you found comfort there, for days on end, and there were no further questions. The need for such questions, it seemed, had quite fallen away. We – just the two of us – were happily settled. And only a gentle skim of house dust came between us. Soon wafted away.

CXCVII

I am standing perpendicular today, greeting each and every one of them with outstretched hand. They do not regard it as any kind of a miracle when I present myself in front of them in this way, and yet it is a miracle, I would have them know that, and yet not in so many words because I have a duty to preserve my dignity. They do not see me when I crawl on all fours about my spaces, the upper and the lower; when I reach out for a chair to help me forward; when I struggle to suck in the next mouthful of life-affirming, life-giving air. If is often so difficult to find the next breath of air in this house. I move about, so slowly, so stealthily, as if I fear that I might spring out and surprise myself down there, forehead almost grazing the boards, reaching forward with first one hand and then another. It is a kind of slow swimming motion that I make, and it causes me to smile just to think of it. And then, at a certain moment of a certain hour, having carefully consulted the clock, I push myself up to my knees, I steady myself, and then I shout out loud for all of me to hear and to heed... One, two, three, and I find that, against all odds, I have succeeded again. I am standing upright, swaying, in the air, doggedly columnar again, and they are all there waiting for me, thinly applauding, and waiting to grasp hold of my hand.

CXCVIII

Let it not be like this again. Let me not find myself in this way. Let me not lose myself in this way. And yet there is no other way. I run in the well settled grooves of myself. I shift between one thing and then another with such ease, all this losing and finding. I am subject to such vicissitudes that I often barely recognise myself from moment to moment. I come and I go. I play hide and seek with myself. The only dependabilities in this life of mine are these few random objects with which I have surrounded myself, and yet they had lives of their own before I even existed, and they will survive long after me unless I choose to wreak vengeance upon them out of sheer madness. They are, in short, and in spite of all that I might wish to fondly believe, wholly indifferent to me or to my needs. It is I alone who invest them with meaning, who make believe that they take pleasure in giving me comfort and succour. Take this bowl, for example. See how it regards me so coldly from the table. Even when it is full to the brim with the warmth of coffee, if is I who have filled it to the brim, it is I who am enfolding it, almost

prayerfully, with my own hands, as if it were a body to be embraced and not this mere indifferent thing.

CXCIX

It is a merest nothing to be walking like this, from bed to table, from door to gate. And yet it is still a miracle of sorts. I understand only now that I have not spent my days reflecting upon this fact, and I know this for a lack. In fact, I have done nothing but move blindly ahead as though life itself were nothing but a dumb, ingenious mechanism of sorts. And then at some point – when exactly? – I must have stopped short, as if on the edge of some terrible abyss. I must have looked down then, vertiginously, and begun at last to reflect upon it all. That by some means or other it had all been set in motion, not only these legs of mine but all those other legs too, and I began to see them all there, out there in that great panjandrum of the street, and to observe how they deftly swerved away from each other upon approach. It was perhaps a divine ballet of sorts, conducted on occasions so humble and so everyday, this life of mine, and all those other lives too, all crowding together in this way... I was quickened then, made ready for everything that was to come in the future, by which I mean the rest of my abundant life, this strange gift newly thrown down at my feet.

CC

Where then if not here? Why this? The questions bounce around me like some game played by a child on a street, and each one is thirsting for an answer. Meanwhile, I take myself off, busyingly, to peer into every convenient hole, here and elsewhere within the bounds of this property. I am no trespasser. I open every book on this desk. I even stare into the depths of my coffee bowl. Fragments, splinters of sound reach me, buoyed up on the air. It is the soughing of the wind. It is the crepitation of booted footsteps on gravel. It is the high piping of some excitable small bird new landed in the fig tree. I go to assemble meaning from each and every one of them. I gather each one up as if in a net, and I spill them out upon this table top as if they were a precious gathering of amber beads. And plucking up each one between thumb and finger, I thread them all on this length of fine spun cotton until I have sufficient to make a pendant of sorts for my neck. I arrange it there in front of this ever patient mirror, and as I sway my body from side to side, I listen to that gaggle of manifold solutions to the riddle of my charmed life.

CCI

Not to be hazarding any more. To have it all spread here in front of me then, becalmed and settled, quite delectably, like some calm and level shore. To smooth the bed sheets over me as if soothing the violence of the sea, expelling those Pharaohs from this land of mine. To have the authority to do so. To know as much as needs to be known, and not to disclose it all, not all at once, not necessarily. To eke it out, little by little, all this knowledge, all this wisdom, Sunday by Sunday, and to see them all gaping up at me in wonderment. I am not after all the sham, the makeweight, the sack of empty air, that I have often believed myself to be. My acuteness is my acuteness, my bodily strength is quite as much as it needs to be. And it does not need to be overmuch. Sufficient unto this new day, that is what I am always telling myself, once and then again. See how the joints of these fingers are still flexing. See how my knees rise to make new hillocks of this bed sheet. See how imperiously I peer out at this new light of dawn. See with what ease I open my mouth and emit the first pure notes of the day. Let the bladder wait a while longer. I am in holy communion with everything that surrounds me.

CCII

The darkest of dark days. The mind and its gropings. God is not within my understanding. He is beyond the door. When I raise my eyes to him, He eludes me. He turns away. He is deep in conversation elsewhere. He is attending to more pressing matters, matters of this universe of ours needless to say. And so when I say His name out loud, I do so hypocritically because I am speaking of some stranger who has fallen out of love with me or who no longer acknowledges me. I wonder what exactly has fallen away, what I have lost, what I so palpably lack. I examine every part of me, the least infirmity. No better and no worse, I conclude. No taller, yet perhaps a little shorter. Every word that I have always used of Him I continue to use, and now those words are turning upon me like so many parasites which have slumbered overlong in the body. They are accusatory. They question my degree of commitment when I go to utter them. I ask them: who is to blame for any of this? I am trying to breathe new life into you, words. I am struggling to believe. Who has emptied them of all meaning? Who is punishing me in this way, and for what particular reason?

CCIII

Incrementally. A tiny shaft of light on the mouse droppings in this corner beside the window. The light has fallen in a very particular way this morning. It is a cleansing light, soft, placable, gently embracing. It weighs upon me, soothingly. Opening the door, and then quickly closing it again. The scoldings of oncoming winter. The thinness of these garments. Insufficient. The evanescence of the body. Paul has reached out to me in the night. I knew him to be there, watching. I have had his presence with me. He tells me to fear for nothing. He advises me, quite firmly, to continue with my life because there is no alternative to this level of confusion and disorder. It is in the nature of things. I pick up my pen and I write

all this down. I am consoled by the sight of the movement of my own hand, so gradual, so bleakly determined. I breathe the breath of this life of mine, steadily.

CCIV

Or not. As the case may be. With all due respect. All these are fencings, posturings, mighty skirmishings of phrases flung out into the air. It is a way of keeping them apart from me, of saying: you are there and I am here. We must both recognise this gulf of ever thickening air which hangs between us. Not to step across. Not to come between. Not to pass through, as if with bodily ease. There is no such thing as bodily ease. The body is slow, stunted, and so reluctant to claim its new place. Let the old places – the old spaces – survive and console. And, meanwhile, to embrace the dumbness of this book which I clasp to my waist. It mews at me. It mewls. And occasionally it even gently chatters as if teasing me with its semblance of small talk. I go to speak back to it. I throw back at it the very words it has offered up to me. Very few of them, it has to be said. The same words go around and around, dizzyingly. I see them, spinning in front of me in the air, a whirligig thrown for a child, to distract him, delight him. I snatch each one out of the air. I go to place it back, with extreme care. Each one has its appointed slot, its groove, its position, its moment, in this book of good orderliness which is clasped to my waist, its home.

CCV

When the moment comes, I shall be ready. I know that I shall have been forewarned, though not in so many words. All my gestures will be prepared, phrases well honed, face set. No one will surprise me in the act of doing unusual or wholly inappropriate things. I will not be caught, bent over, raking grey ash from the grate into the bucket. There will be no pother of dust rising up into my face when the moment comes. My face will not be smeary. I will not be coughing deep-throatedly. There will be no clattering or clashing of dishes at the sink. My hands will not be water-slippery. They will be dry, bony, and as still as the air just then, which will have calmed. There will be such an unusual degree of calmness. I will not be standing at the door, waiting, peering out. That would be to over-anticipate to a ridiculous degree. That would be to guess at the hour of his coming, which would be an act of brazen impertinence. All the same, and in spite of my best self-cautionings, I do feel that I will know exactly how and when and where it will be. I will be seated here at my desk, staring down at these words which I have just written. I will be poised, so attentive, between one apposite phrase and then another. Paul will have made an intervention. He will have set me at a certain angle to myself. He will know exactly, as always, what there is to be teased out of me. Yes, I know that he will be closer than close just before it happens. And then, when I turn my head to look for him again, perhaps in order to thank him, perhaps merely to acknowledge his presence near me once again, as it has always been, I will find him absent. And at that exact moment of his absence, in the immediate aftermath of that turn of the head in his direction, having recognised, for the first and last time of all, that he is not there, and that he will not be there ever again because his time is over and done, once and for all, it will happen. And I believe that I will not be dissatisfied with the final outcome. I believe that I will experience then, just as it is happening, more than a modicum of contentment. I will harbour no wistfulness. I will not be of a maudlin disposition. I will not be speaking evil of myself.

CCVI

I fight through these days of mine. I say to myself, and in spite of all yearnings to the contrary: these days of mine are not to be rejected because they are so carefully numbered. And yet I often find myself on the brink of rejecting them. They can be so foul-mouthed, so refractory, so resistant to my least little wish. And I speak not of people – these days of mine are seldom peopled – but of the wind, the rising wind, the rain, the mercilessly beating rain, the very blackness, the very louringness, of the clouds, which hang down like black sacks of doom above my head. When I see them again through the fogged panes of my upstairs window, bearing down upon me, I feel inclined to retire to my bed, to pull the blanket over my head, to close my eyes in order to dream again. But I do not dream. I cannot dream. The wind, its soughing, its heavy breathing, the way it makes the walls shake and shudder, comes between me and my dreams. There is one answer, and I pledge to myself, there and then, that I must apply that answer. I rise up again. I dress myself. I clatter down the stairs, face set against the enormities, the cruelties, the miseries of it all, and then, having flung back the door in order to experience it on my face, my neck – how it drizzles down my neck! – my hands, I bellow so loudly that no one would credit that I had such capacity in these old and shrunken lungs of mine.

CCVII

There are always, thank goodness, moments between these moments of distress, when I am walking, so lightly and so tenderly, in my garden, small though it may be, back and forth, hand in hand with myself. And the voices of the many border flowers are speaking up at me, describing, with such touching modesty, their changeability, remarking upon the fact that they are no sooner blooming than blown. A great sadness seizes hold of me then. I kneel down. I speak back to them. I cup one, so carefully, the one which seems to be paying me particular attention. There is always one. The others often indulge in a species of feigning, which can be maddening. I look deep into its face. I remark upon our kinship. I remind it that we are almost at one in the way that we flourish and

then fade. It makes no comment upon my words. It merely nods, and then quickly inclines its head towards sleep.

CCVIII

On each new morning, I grasp hold of this life of mine, quite roughly, as if by the scruff of the neck. I say to it, almost shrieking, as if my clothes have caught fire from that wood stove down in the kitchen: go or come, and come quickly! Do not hesitate for a single second! I skitter, March-hare mad, around from place to place within this room, swerving and turning about, like an hysterical bridegroom dancing himself into a state of near unconscious bliss on the morning of his life's great renewal, desperately striving to see anew, to burnish and to vivify each old thing. I squeeze my nose up against the glass of the window in order to recognise, with yelps of pleasure, each new minted day of spring, summer, winter, as the case may be. Is this not then new? I ask myself, shrilling. It requires such goading on my part, all this putting of the self through its paces. For the fact is that I have no wish to see it all again. And yet I also have this overwhelming urge to make it all anew, everything that there is in this straitened world of mine, by which I mean everything which exists within the ever narrowing span of my gaze, because there is nothing other than this. There is nothing else ahead of me on this day other than that clotted mist of sorts which hangs between the trees down in the valley, ragged and ghostly as an old palmer's weeds. I see myself now running into those trees, flailing my arms, embracing thrilling new worlds of lostness, in which I no longer know myself for what or who I am any more, or in which direction I am said to be travelling. New excitements, new voices assail me until, in the end, when I am utterly spent at day's end, dragging myself ahead on my knees, I recognise them to be the old voices, tricksily veiled and disguised somewhat. The past is a prankster. It is always playing the same old tricks on me. I am growing so tired of my life. The taste of if all is so sour on the tongue's tip.

CCIX

He has arrived without warning. He has settled himself. He has come to ask me a few questions. Not many questions, he lies. His words slip down the side of his mouth like a thin black snake. I prepare myself on this chair, my chair, beside the window. The sun has been smiling weakly on the back of my neck. When I put my hands down upon its two old wooden arms, it seems to want to reassure me. It presses its back against my back, as if to say to me: stay staunch. I will always be behind you. I have shaped myself to this chair. It has happened over a matter of years, this slow coming together. It loves me. It soothes me. It watches over me like a mother might have done. It does not move when I ask it to remain stock still, tucked half beneath this desk of mine. When I blink awake, it is still patiently waiting for me. It will never not wait for me. It is the last thing that I touch at nights. That touch, so seemingly casual, always reassures me. I see the impress of myself, of my twin buttocks, ever thinning these days, in its weary and dependable seat, in the dimpling of its leather, the way it has always sagged so to receive me, as if it knew exactly my weight, my proportions, what exactly would be demanded of it on this day or any other. And so when he begins to speak to me, when he describes to me, so levelly, the extent of the questions that he will be putting to me, one after another, without so much as a breathing space, and tells me how deeply into my life they will probe, and how perhaps, in the fullness of time, he may yet eviscerate me, I do something quite simple. I say to my chair, my friend and dearest companion: please answer for me. And there is by way of immediate response a barely discernible creak of reassurance.

CCX

Wait a moment, please. I do not have to tell you any of this – no one has asked me to do so – but I shall do so anyway. I have set

down this account in the most casual way possible. There has been no preparation – just as no one prepared me to live this life of mine. I slithered out by accident, bawling at the top of my voice, and then everything began for me. Similarly, these words of mine that you have been reading have been as unpremeditated as water spewing from the mouth of a gargoyle, risen up there so high in the air. Day after day I have set down my least thoughts as another man might have chosen to lift a finger and, for no good reason at all, stare and stare at it until he went dizzy. This is exactly the way in which I have proceeded. I am by no means a literary man, as I have already told you. I have no beguiling yarns to spin about my life. I have no luscious words of deceit in which to enmesh you until you squeal with delight. I have no carefully crafted narrative to unfold. All I have, tumbled out like broken toys from a sack in some attic, are these bits and pieces of my life, and I must now ask you to forgive me if you began by expecting more of me. I did not offer you more than this. Do not say that I did not warn you, right at the beginning of our journey. And do not forget also that I took Paul as my example, and that it is he who is responsible for the fact that I have set out at all upon this journey, which seldom gives me much pleasure. I am doing it for his sake, you must understand. I ask you then to forgive me for being myself. I ask you to stop now if you are already weary to the point of acute exasperation.

CCXI

Marie has a particular way of goading me. It is the way that she hums, so deep in her throat, when she circles the kitchen table as she waxes its pitted and uneven surface. I hear it as I sit here at my desk upstairs, preparing myself to meet the day, preparing to gather the words which will set in motion that mighty, life-long effort to explain me to myself. It is my only task, as it was Paul's before me: to calculate, as though mathematically (yes, as precisely as that), the length and the depth and the breadth of myself; to discover of what exactly I consist. And then her maddening humming begins, sawing down through the air. It is not exactly the sound of bees in the garden. That can be so deliciously mind-numbing, and especially so during the long, slow months of summer. I see myself riding the air with them, sucking at their nectar. No, hers is of a different kind altogether. It is a constant, wheedling drone which comes between me and my thinking. When I hear it again – and she always carries it with her – my mind fogs over and my hands begin to tremble. I watch myself rising up from my chair to almost twice my natural height, and then descending the stairs in a mood of near uncontrollable fury. I stand in front of her, bellowing at her, screwing my hands together as I speak to her. She stands before me, squeezed back against the sink, head bowed, so contrite, saying nothing. Globby tears are welling from her eyes. I raise my hand. I watch it rising, as if of its own accord. At that point, seated as I am at my desk upstairs, I distract myself from this vision of such an act of uncharacteristic unpleasantness by staring hard at a spider's web which, day by day, has been growing in luxuriousness in the far upper corner of the window. I have taken delight in such arabesques, always.

CCXII

Where else then am I to travel? You tell me, know-alls. It seems to myself – and who better to know the truth of myself than I? – that I have travelled everywhere. My incessant journeyings have exhausted me, utterly. When I stare at the thinness of my face in this glass, I know this for an incontrovertible truth, that I have been amongst the world's great adventurers. In my mind I have seen it all and more: Van Diemen's Land; Honduras; the plains of Patagonia; the golden domes of Kiev; the wastes of Siberia... Where else is there to go? The creatures of this village, which is my more than world, laugh at me to hear it, of course, because they do not understand that to travel is to spin on the point of a pin for thousand upon thousand of miles. Such dizzying distances! Yes, I have travelled inside myself, that has been my lifelong journey, as it was Paul's before me. And it will forever continue until I reach that point of no return. And I am so satisfied by all of this. No creature of flesh and blood could be more so. I have no desire to squat me down on the severed foot of an elephant. I carry all my maps within me.

CCXIII

I kneel at my bedside this evening for a very particular purpose. I am teaching myself to sing in order to give thanks for all of this, to acknowledge this world which surrounds me like a great and ever expanding gift, flung out from here, from field to coppice to farmstead, as far as the farthest beyondness. Yes, I have at last reached this point in my life's adventure. I have always been so muted when the organ notes, ever swelling, have risen to a great diapason. I have opened my mouth, as if in homage, but in fact not a single sound has ever been emitted. I have always – and I say it to my shame – been feigning. Until now. Now I am opening my mouth and listening out for my first notes. Who in this world would have guessed it? It is so low, so deep in the throat, so tremulously tentative and even child-like in its fearfulness. Will I ever find a greater courage? Patience, I say to myself, patience. I hold this low note for minutes on end, and as I do so, I see the insects gathering about my feet in wonder and admiration co-mingled, the carpet beetles, the spider fresh swung down from the window corner, and even the common fly or the flea from my sleeve, they are all here, come to join me, and perhaps even to encourage my efforts. They offer up to me their own various harmonics, which consists of a scattering of sounds from thin to waveringly expansive. We chorus together. And then, as my voice gains courage to rise and to rise, I hear other voices gathering just beyond the door. It is the sound of bird song now. The songbirds are at the door. We are all in this together.

CCXIV

My thoughts intermingle, intermesh with yours as water mingles with water in this sink. I step out without you, wholly alone and upstanding, and then I notice, by the casting of a shadow, that you are walking in step with me. Our voices, so often, feel like twin murmurations, so deftly are they intertwined. I start this new sentence now, and I know, by the ease with which it is done, that you have completed it for me. I experience then a kind of easefulness within because I know that you are stockaded about me, protecting me from the worst of things. But can there really truly be any worst of things in this small and truncated world of mine? Am I not exaggerating? Alas, it is all too true. That worst is when I fall headlong into myself oh much too far for comfort, when I recognise myself to be someone wholly other than what I had always imagined myself to be. It is at such troubling times as these that you walk with me on my journey. And yet you too are other to me. How could you not be? You are not a part of me. And yet I know that, in part at least, to be an untruth.

CCXV

They have stopped, all at once, in unison, as if on cue, all the people of this village, and all so dimly known to me. I have been walking ahead of them, steadily, and with all due solemnity, through the fields, and we have all been chanting those familiar words in praise of Him. He has been carried between us, raised up on his bier, holding his rosary, fingering it. And I have been saying out loud various prayers in his honour. It is what we all must do, always, on this day of the year, to remember Him as he once was, to remember how he fell – how he was felled, like a mighty tree – struck down by that volley of sticks and stones, and how his blood splattered across the thirsty ground. We all think back, heads bowed, to that spreading stain, and how, in an instant, it immortalised and sacralised his name. We embrace it in our hearts. We swim in it. We almost drown in it, such is our devotion to his memory. We think of our own heart's blood, and of how little and insufficient it seems to be as an offering. Nevertheless, it is all that we have, and we readily, eagerly offer it up to him, and he accepts it, just as readily. He drinks it. We see him drinking it down, each and every offering, one by one, in the eye of the mind. We continue to walk on, and then, at a certain point on the journey, we set him down, with all due reverence and solemnity, beside the field, where the cows still steam with curiosity. And then they turn to me. Cricking my neck, I look up beyond, to where the stars are beginning to appear, one by one, as if by some magical gift, in the evening sky. And then I let the silence settle until that moment of truth arrives where they wait for my words of explanation and consolation for his suffering and, less so, for our own. I go to reach out for those words. I feel my fingers scurrying. I feel them emerging, so thinly spread, and yet they are more than sufficient.

CCXVI

I bore myself terribly in the repeating over to myself all these nagging frustrations. You too, I have no doubts about that. The problem is always this. I cannot truly do because I am always waiting to do. I cannot invest this single moment fully with meaning because it is always on the brink of being superseded by something a little better, a little more significant, a little clearer and more fully formed, a little more meaningful perhaps. And so it is that I always find myself poised here, on this step or this stair, preparing to do battle or perhaps preparing to learn some lesson appertaining to a greater cause than this one. In short, this passing, fleeting moment does not seem quite sufficient unto itself. It always feels like a lesser thing, a mild disappointment, happened upon at an unexpected turning; a promise perhaps, a foggy aspiration of sorts, a preparing

to be that distant and perhaps marvellous someone whose nature has not yet been revealed to me. And here I must stand then, fully honed and ready, fully prepared for the next eventuality, a bow taut-strung, poised here on the dizzying precipice of each new morning. Oh, would that I could know myself truly, see through this maddening, muffling mist of confusion, to the final end of things! If only this moment were to be the last of its kind, a kind of culminating triumph, when all the books were finally to be closed, and all the dust settled once and for all. And yet I know that it is not so. Life gapes open ahead of me, formlessly. I see that again today as I stare out through this smeary window. And still I go blundering on, yelping, running back and forth, tail-chasing. Helplessly. Hopelessly.

CCXVII

I have gone, without saying goodbye. That would be needless. No one would be listening. I am not, for the most part, a figure of public curiosity. I have left the key hidden in a crevice, side on, behind the tallest of the hollyhocks. I am carrying little with me, a small portmanteau with my night things, a change of clothes, and an assortment of necessary texts with which to embolden me in the future. If is not too heavy. I do not toil beneath its weight. I walk across the grass, head bowed, even-paced, in the shadow of the chancel. I do not look up. I am not about to pay heed to all these random, circumambient voices.

CCXVIII

A death. A death. There has been a great and incontrovertible death. In my heart I know it now, as I have known nothing else with such certainty in the whole of my life, that my Paul is dead. And their Paul too, of course, though I am inclined to admit to that reluctantly. Do they have claims upon him, these people? Have they ever known him for who he is? Are they anything other than passing familiar with his name? The air outside is thick with it. They are saying that it is so in the streets. Even at the *Mairie* they are whispering his name, as amongst those who have passed away, officially, telling me, with such glowing, prideful eyes, of the triumphant solemnity of his leaving this world, and of how the crowds massed on the boulevards of Paris as the funeral *cortège* passed by, so slowly, with its eight black, plumed horses, not one of them restive – it was as though they knew the solemnity of this occasion – pulling his casket. And I, I was not even present there bodily, I said to myself as I listened to those words. I was buried here, unaware, asleep in this village, this nowhere, when, elsewhere, it was all going on... And here I come now, running after, ashamed, knowing nothing about it until this morning, when I awoke and – just then, at the point of waking, as if stabbed by the news – knew it to be true. It was in the air, encircling me, the story of his death. And when I walked out into the garden like a man possessed, it was everywhere about me. The songbirds were all mute today. The bees remained hidden away in their hives, unstirring. The hollyhocks hung their heads beside the garden gate, and even the leaves of the lavender, when I pinched them between thumb and finger, had lost their familiar savour. He is dead then. He is gone away.

CCXIX

And yet some intimate – perhaps it is the most intimate – part of me knows none of this to be true, and yet I dare not say as much out loud in the streets of this village for fear of causing consternation and disbelief. And so I must say it to myself, within the confines of the walls of this house: Paul is not dead. He is merely feigning a death like a brilliant prestidigitator of sorts. He cannot die. It would be a miracle for him to die, a miracle beyond even God's encompassing. I know that for a fact when I take up his

books, one by one, from this table top, and read his words over to myself again. They are the words of a man young in heart, vibrant, fresh stepping out, with such boldness and confidence, into the world of the spirit. And when I go to read them out loud, as I do this morning, at the top of my voice, as if brandishing them, with such defiance, in the teeth of his death, that feigned death, I hear him begin to read them after me, in that familiar voice of his, in a kind of soothing after-echo of that voice of his... There is no question of it then. His death was all an illusion, all that pageantry. He is still here with me, sitting so comfortable and secure in this chair of mine, wreathed in his aromatic pipe smoke, investigating the mysteries of the Self, and even writing the occasional line of poetry. He cannot but be alive, I am telling myself, over and over, almost chanting the words, as long as I myself am alive to witness all of this. I pinch myself. I stand before the glass. I clench my two fists. I acknowledge this fact: there are just the two of us. It is more than enough. It is life full and brimming over.

CCXX

A stunned, heavy silence in this room. The weighing down of an oppressive heat. Such an ever tightening constriction of the throat. Close to gagging. I reach out for the water glass. It is almost empty. There is a fly swimming, idling through its death throes, in the shallows. I set it down with such impatience, such violence, almost breaking it. If would have been good to break it. It would not have been good to make my feet bleed by stepping out amongst the cruelties of a random strewing of glass shards. A dull, full-to-bursting throbbing at the temples. It is as though my heart, pulsing, is alive now in these temples of mine, giving such pain, causing such thunderous noises. I lie on my back, and I strive to float a little. Clenching my teeth, I manage to rise an inch or so up from my bed, and then I fall back again, heavily, stinking, like a filthy hessian sack of animal waste. Have I ever been so helpless, so repulsive to myself? I try flexing the joints of my fingers. They feel strangely set apart from me, ancient relics from some casket in a dusty chancel. I stretch them. Now they are about to be offered to one more needy. Should I release them? Will I not need them? I endeavour to set out upon this daily journey of my thinking. It is all so wearisome and so worthless. Nothing can emerge from this nothing which is the self. I find myself arriving at a door, almost immediately, a locked door without a key. I thunder upon that door until I make my fists bleed. I slump down upon the threshold of stone, feeling its coldness ripple up through my spine. Can all this begin again? I ask myself in a voice which sounds so distant, so strangely unfamiliar. Has it the strength to begin again? Will he ever be here again with me?

CCXXI

I blame him for it all, this entrapment that I must wake to, daily. The past is entirely expunged, Paul has said that to me, repeatedly. The words thrum, din, in the inner ear. Consider, and then discard, the dross of memory. He has encouraged me to think in this way. Each moment is to be fresh made anew. And there is nothing else that I can embrace as my own. I have the right to claim nothing but this. My future resides in it, that I must begin again, to name it all, all that is yet to exist within my ken, in the freshness of this new space, to call it all back into being. And yet the task is an impossible one because I lack the wherewithal to recognise what it is that I must see. I lack the words with which to name that which must be named. I am a dumb, unseeing beast. Am I even that? Have I even been conjured into being? I am asking myself. Is this existence to which I refer merely a dream of itself? I am nothing but a possibility of the I that is yet to be revealed. To whom though? How am I to be revealed to myself when I lack the means to do so? I lie here, a lumpish mass, waiting to be shaped and quickened by that which shall perhaps remain forever nameless. There is nothing more to be said.

Part Two

CCXXII

I took it up in my hands this morning, this book of the story of his childhood. It was not my childhood. I began to inveigle myself, to walk beside him when he walked, to mimic his gestures, to talk in his voice. There was no love lost. He even put a little distance between us as we walked. Instead of looking at me when he turned to acknowledge me, he seemed to be looking through me, as if I did not belong there, in his life, at that moment on the journey of his life. It was as if I had inserted myself with violence. I stopped then. I let him walk on. I even let the book fall from my hand, quite roughly, as it had never done before. Then I lifted up my eyes again, to the fields, to the barn, outside the window. I saw how the light was trembling this morning, as if unsure of itself. It was a strangely darkened and bruised light, a light of no particular moment, in this day or any other. I tried to insert myself into that light. I tried to belong to this day of which I was surely a part. I could not do so. Some part of me was still staring after him as he walked ahead of me. Some part of me was still remonstrating with him for being so cruel to me. Some part of me could not accept that I had flung that book down upon the table top, that I in my turn had gone through the heart-breaking motions of rejecting him in my turn. Where am I ever to be if I am not here now? Where was I ever to be if I was not there then?

CCXXIII

Yes, it is as ever. How could it not be as ever? The gestures are customary, and they flow in various directions, sometimes jaggedly, in order to catch at the corner of the eye. I rise and then I fall. I go to reach out, with the utmost tentativeness, and then I draw myself in again, quite quickly. I move myself forward like a great and cumbersome vessel, with a certain belling, swelling motion, as if by way of tribute to my presence here. As if I were a gift, not lightly to be dismissed. Ridiculous, of course. They have a certain way of looking at me. Side on. Askance. Dry of mouth. As if both looking and not looking. Curiously incurious and a touch fearful, as if I might give off sparks. I step out in order to do the simplest thing in the world, the most common thing. To buy milk from the *épicerie*, for example. I let the small coins dribble from my finger ends as if I am playing a child's game with pretty mademoiselle, the daughter. She was standing there just now, waiting for my approach, a little stiffer than need be, as if preparing herself to undergo some small ordeal. Her limbs had to be just so. I have known her all my life. I remember how she kicked earth at me as a child, though not deliberately. She treats me with the same degree of respectful fearfulness. What am I to say of any of this? I am who I am. I have chosen my life. I have been chosen by my life. I cannot but continue to fall into this unfathomable abyss of myself. Nor can she fail to look at me, somewhat at least, when I go to pay her the pittance for the little that she gives me. She does so, glancingly, as if to come near me is to suffer pain of a kind not easily to be described. I suffer that pain too, in my turn. I too am an awkward, fearful assemblage of gristle, blood, bone. I do not tell her that. There are idle murmurings at my back. I do not try to listen. I know that no one is trying to speak to me. There are no topics of conversation between us. There never could be. There could never be an occasion, in this place, when I would be due to be spoken to. And that both displeases me and pleases me to no small degree. I nod. I smile. I pass on. They are not wholly unhappy that I am amongst them. They are not unwelcoming. I belong to the ancient fabric of this place. I am a part of their rootedness, their memory. I give them succour, of sorts. When they look at me, they think this: I am falling short. This man knows me. This man sees into me. He judges me. All nonsense, of course. I know so little. And it lessens and lessens by the hour. Life streams away from me by the hour, the minute.

CCXXIV

This bale of twine here, living in this box, it so readily reminds me of myself, how it unravels and unravels when I let it fall across the floor, bouncing away from me, ever more desperately, ever more skittishly, running away from itself. It is so thin when flung out like this. It barely has substance at all. I bend down to it. I cut off a length, quite carelessly, before flinging it away from me again. It barely exists, except when it is needed, as it is today, to bundle up some newspapers. Then it comes into its own. It demonstrates to me its properties of strength and endurance. I feel, when I wrap it around my hand, what harm it could cause, when tightened around a man's neck, how it would make the difference between life and death. It is then that I ball it up again, in a hurry.

CCXXV

My body consists of these manifold warring elements. I lie here, trying to bring peace to that which will not be at peace, to that which refuses to be calmed, quelled or appeased. And I am not speaking here of bodily pain, the pain that one suffers when the stomach rejects foodstuffs, causing it to bend over in agony, to retch, to expectorate into the bowl. All that is purely of the body and its routine mechanisms. I speak rather of our rearing, tearing moods, of how our character insists upon turning and turning about. We thrash about in the dark, not knowing who or what we are. We believe ourselves to be this, and then, moments later, we prove to be that. And there is no end to any of this. We connive at our own treachery. There is no calming, it seems, these boiling seas of contradiction.

CCXXVI

I had dreamt otherwise, of a movement so sacred. There is no serenity about any of this. It is all so much horror and panic. When I rise, I find myself moving too quickly. My body is sucked up into the air at such a dizzying speed that no part of me is within my control. I have lost hold of myself. My arms thrash around me in the freezing air. My legs lash out in all directions, aiming to do violence to nothing at all. There is no sense and no understanding any more. All my faculties have left me. All coherence has gone. I am bibbly-babbling at no one. Parts of my body appear to be falling away from me. I cannot see through these eyes of mine. Can this really be some heavenly haven towards which I am ascending?

CCXXVII

Light again, stepping-slow and congenial, it has to be said. Let me say it out loud then, in the presence of this complaisant morning air, if only to cheer myself with my own words. There is not so far to go today. I know that. I am measuring the distances. I can encompass them, so easily, with my eye. I take it evenly, dull, soft, tentative footfall by dull, soft, tentative footfall, down the steps to the garden, and then I turn towards the fig tree, a full, swivelling turn. I am, as ever, watchful of myself. I am my sole preoccupation. A gift of unknowing, flung from out of the dark. Oh how I tease myself. The moments are easing their way along so carefully today, and so soothing calmly, one by one, as are the clouds above this head of mine, which have now formed a sort of protective canopy over me for reasons which must forever remain unfathomable. There is a mood of somnolence today, everywhere. Even the few people that I see are intent upon almost nothing, and very painstakingly, very gradually. Each one of them seems to be walking with tiny steps, as if perhaps fearful of a sudden noise, akin to some animal's unnerving screech, at dusk, from the nearby wood. They are all biding their time, quietly wishing the day away. Each one is counting the beats of his own heart, though not obsessively. Each heart is like a tender, lulling drum of sorts, companionable. In short, they are all hanging back inside themselves. Just as I too hang back inside myself, having no wish to hazard. The day is too tame and too peaceable for hazarding. I try to divest myself of all my words, to shed them one by one as I walk, like so many stones thrown down carelessly, and as if unthinkingly. I do this because I know them to have been over-used, and now it is time to shed them. I must return myself to the simplicity of as little as possible. That is what the world seems to require of me today. That is why it is staring at me, so steadily, in the way that it is. It is surely urging me to live as simply as I must surely know how, unhurriedly, unknowingly. Not to experience all that hullabaloo again. There has been too much of all of that. It has been that and nothing else for as long as I can permit myself to remember. It has sickened me to the point of a desperate lust for sudden departure. Let me then expunge it all now, as the blackboard was once wiped clean in the schoolroom with a few deft sideways strokes of the rag. And then we can all begin again, with such a promise of child-like bright-shiningness.

CCXXVIII

Dearly beloved, I am addressing these few words to you because you are here with me, inside my voice, like a welcome lodger in this house of mine. You are at one with me. When I come and go – anywhere that I so choose – you always walk with me. Your friendship is not in doubt. And yet today, it seems to me, I say all this falsely, because nothing is secure inside these fragile walls of me, and least of all you. Everyone is looking in at me. Was it not once your task, and even your promise, to stand between, to bear the brunt of their hostilities? If so, where exactly are you? You are here, you say, and then you seem to fade again as voices fade when they retreat from me. You do this at such maddening moments, when your sentences are half finished. I hang on your words, which do not arrive. And then when I ask you to address me in your turn, you remain quizzically silent, as if picking apart the least little request that I have put to you, measuring its inadequacies in the great scheme of things... I called you dearly beloved just now because those are the words that I have always used when addressing you, but can they really be true? Are you really dear to me, and I to you? Are you beloved on this day too?

CCXXIX

It is being offered to me, on this day as any other. I see the hands holding it out. I stretch out my own hands to receive it. It is the gift of goodness. I would offer it to them, offer it in my turn as I have been offered it. That is the way of things. They step up enthusiastically. They receive the box with all eagerness. They hang over it, tearing at the wrapping. Then they lift the lid. They stare and they stare. Then each one reaches in and lifts out a tiny part of it, so carefully, in order not to cause harm. They stand there, shaking, uncomprehending, tearful. I try to explain. I try to offer them some measure of appeasement. I do not myself understand, I tell them, why that perfect mirror should have shattered into so many pieces.

CCXXX

There can be nothing quite as terrible as this, I am thinking to myself as I walk, eyes fixed to the uneven ground on this gusting, rainy morning lest I slip or I slide, to witness it at the last, as some indifferent outsider might witness it in my stead, the slow dissolution of the self. Or will it not be slow? Will it not after all be as quick as the descent of a knife to the heart? Who is to say or to know? First those years of long decay, and then the slipping away into nothingness. The final unmaking of all that was so carefully made down the long years of earthly endurance. Yes, to unmake all that was made, with such loving attention. To unmask all that was masked. But before that, perhaps to stand there, naked, in shivering readiness, with nothing to be pleaded for, no more farewells to be said. To yield up the self as one might idly toss aside a long loved and well used garment, without a thought to the contrary, without a thought that this garment might be tested against the flames, wholly consumed and yet, by some miracle, remain still intact, moulded, shaped, renewed, yes, after all made anew by those purging flames. Otherwise, there can be no defining consummation, and all talk of this or any other kind is surely in vain, and I push ahead now, step by defining step, for no good reason.

CCXXXI

It is in the dead hours of yet another early afternoon – how can I have counted up so many? – that I am walking down this oh so familiar lane with the same degree of headlong compulsion. My eyes are ranging ahead of me, looking to left and to right as they go, desperately seeking out proof, as if they were torches held in the hand, flaring in the dark of the night. Some part of me yearns to shout out loud in defiance of all that I have, oh so many times, seen and accepted and even known to be true (though not fully, it has to be said): this is not what happened at all! Once again, some part of me is jesting. No, harsher still: I am lying to myself. For the truth is that the walls of the old cow byre have indeed fallen in on themselves, as if giving up the ghost. I see it all once again, as I walk downhill in its direction, strewn across lane and field immediately at its back, evidence of all that ruination, and then I gain speed, I hurry on by, as if I cannot bear to stay for a single second longer. What is the reason for all this hurrying? I am not yearning to arrive. No one is waiting for me. It is so seldom that anyone is ever

waiting for me in this world. I stop myself. I walk back a few paces. I look again. I seek to calm and to clarify my feverish thinking. I examine each fallen stone, stricken once again by the fact that it is gone, snatched away by a storm when, wholly unheeding, I was sleeping the sleep of the unknowing. I try to screw my eyes tight shut, but I cannot stop myself seeing all of this. It sticks to me like a burr. I force myself to turn away, to look away from it, as if I am chastising a small child. I walk on – or I will never walk on. Who then is driving all this walking? And when I arrive at last, in no time at all, at the entrance, I recognise myself with a shock of wonderment. I see that I am already there, a dragonfly at the height of summer, skimming, zig-zagging as I go, across the surface of the water, almost touching. I am mesmerised by the sight of me here, combing and combing its surface, reduced, at the height of summer, to nothing but this, to these few swinging and darting and swift-needling gestures of such a lightsomeness and passing ease that I cannot but marvel at how I could exist in this way in the world. Everything is noiseless now. All human clamour has passed away. The wind has gone. The women, who are here of a morning in such numbers, have all been spirited away in the blink of an eye, as if by some genius of the place, taking their fat and lumpish bundles and their incessant idle chatter with them. I seem to see them, idling back up the lane, wending their way, weaving in and out amongst themselves as the conversation leads them. Not a single one of them gives a thought to me, to my compulsions, and of how, now, just a matter of minutes or hours later, I am at peace here, skimming this surface, having had all my burdens removed from me, as I stare down into the depths of this water, somewhat *en passant,* and even a little blurrily. I open my eyes. I take off my shoes. It seems to be the right thing to do, the gesture that is being demanded of me. I sit myself down. I hang my head over the water. I let my feet idle for a moment in all that shocking coldness. Here I am, I whisper to myself (I am well out of earshot), suspended amongst the living and the dead.

<h1 style="text-align:center">CCXXXII</h1>

If this crack in the wall widens sufficiently, I will surely be able to put my foot through it, that goes without saying. Or does it? And so I must wait. I must attend upon it. It is a little to the right of the bed, at the level of the newel post. Days ago, it admitted my wheedling finger end. Now it has grown in ambition. And I am not unduly alarmed, not yet. There are cracks, everywhere, in this house, yet none of them is quite as significant as this one is proving to be. It will be a question, finally, of whether or not I wish to admit the world in its entirety, whether I want the interior of this house and the world beyond to be as one. I have always said no, no, no in the past when this proposition has presented itself to me. There are two quite distinct modalities of being, one experienced on the inside, and the other on the outside. I am not the same here as I am there, nor would I wish to be. And so when I lean down and stare into this crack, and feel, pricking my eye, that faint breath of air coursing through it, and understand how it will gain in speed and forcefulness the more it widens, I must also take on the burden of deciding what exactly, in the days to come, I may wish my life to be, and, needless to say, that is not entirely clear to me.

<h1 style="text-align:center">CCXXXIII</h1>

I hear it like a mighty hammer blow to the side of the head, distant at first and then, as I slowly rise towards consciousness, with greater aural definition. Raining down upon me, remorselessly, mercilessly. Blow after blow after staggering blow. I conjure such meanings as I am able. The great marble head rolls gutter-ward. The temple is felled. Or many another instance plucked from the annals. The ticking of the clock at my side registers these passing moments with such violence. Yet it need not be so, I am telling myself as my hand rises towards it, stilling it, muffling it. Time is a continuum, I tell myself, as the clock inclines its old ear towards me with such patience, all is so untroublingly smooth and utterly divisionless in the eye of the great taskmaster. There are no arbitrary rules to be imposed. I say it again, as if to convince myself: we drift from here to there. And it is all vain pretence, for there is no here and no there. Yesterday bears along with it all the freshness of tomorrow again. I have anticipated myself. I have eavesdropped upon everything that I am yet to do or to be. I have lived my life already, to the full and brimming over. I have died, times innumerable, of weariness, of shame, of decline, of scrofula... There have been so many eager, death-seeking opportunities to be seized. And did I not seize them, and then return, as if by some miracle, zestful, blinking awake? I have experienced the fullness of my future – of, pardon, my futures. And here it all is now, like an ever expandable scroll before my eyes, in all its peacockish, eye-beguiling contemporaneity, always too much of it. And when I see this everything, all at once, I in fact see nothing because there is always too much to be seen. And who is equipped to do this seeing anyway, who stands forth to claim the right to do so? What fragile mechanism rises up, ghost-like, from between these twisted, stinking sheets telling me in a voice so cannily akin to my own that it possesses the wherewithal to contemplate any of this, the ability to bear the known world upon its shoulders? Who is the liar on this day of days, and who the lied to? Sleeping or waking, it is much the same.

CCXXXIV

Am I a hero? Would that be to exaggerate? I bear up his world– such as it is. I sustain. I do nothing but sustain. And so it has always been. Count them up if you so wish, all the individual details of the burden of my life. There are these books – and usually precious little else. I fill this space beside his window, little admired, little noticed. I carry the weight of each one. I bear the weight of each one. This is not a matter of conscience. I am not creaturely. And

then there is the matter of his pen, which is also unbudging at this hour. A table top believes itself to be a thing of no importance, happening to exist in this world because it has been willed into existence by another. Let me say it again: there is no question of guilt, deservingness or curiosity. I am curious about nothing. No spirit stirs within me. I do not carry the burden of a conscience upon my shoulders. And it is for this reason that I find myself fortunate. I know myself to be a thing of the moment. He, on the other hand, is blown, helplessly, between one shore and another. He is a thing subject to judgement, always, and yet he is helpless to judge of his own inadequacies. He cannot take his moments as they come, idly, casually, one by one. He is always crawling desperately back across the past or trying to second-guess a future which he can never know. In short, he is helpless and pitiable, with this intolerable burden of conscience. Whereas I am nothing but helpless and pitiable – if you so wish. If that is how you choose to judge me. Or I can strip it all away. I can divest myself of such qualities. I can be little more than a nothing, to be disposed of at whim. Such is the extent of the freedom of the various conjoined planks of wood which you choose to call a table top.

CCXXXV

The hours are so makeshift. They come and they go, incurious, unheeding. How did they learn such a measure of indifference? Each blink of light is a tiny trap into which I fall. I test my voice on the air. I hear it fade and wither. It is so tuneless. Tunelessly small, and also weak and biddable. Carried wheresoever by the air, the riderless air. Who am I then? Who have I ever sought to be? And who, incidentally, are you? Did I once put this fine distance between just the two of us? I exchanged glances with you once. There was brightness surrounding me on that day, a refulgent, gulping brightness. I was stepping out, beyond the lulling, dulling confinements of the self. I found myself stepping towards you across our level green ground. We seemed to be approaching each other. Our heads were raised, with that wish to entangle. We locked glances, momentarily. I saw myself in your eyes, pitiable. The glances faltered, then fell away. And yet, just a matter of seconds before they did so, I knew that I had reached you. I had snatched you to me. I had questioned you in a thousand different ways, I had pleaded with you, I had offered myself to you, the everything that I have always been and must surely forever be, with a childish degree of solemnity. And yet not a word had been exchanged between us. And still, years on, you lodge with me here, deep within my fastness, and I commune with that which I have retained of you. It all amounts to a fragile hope of sorts, you must understand that. In so far as you are listening.

CCXXXVI

It is as if a voice from afar has proclaimed it, and, without a second's demur, I have nodded my acceptance. And the message is this: there is a certain rightness to the perpendicular. I speak of this table leg, against which my own stout right leg presses itself when I am bowed over this desk, pen in hand. It is a type of pure and uninterrupted Ascension. I feel myself rising with it, on spasmodic eddies of optimism. And yet it is the horizontal which seems to apportion out its regular daily doses of comfort and appeasement. Nothing pleases me more than to lie my head down on this table top, across the lumpish terrain of this familiar scattering of books, and to spread my arms as if in helplessly submissive readiness for all that may eventuate. A helpless posture, yes – but a dependably steady one too. The rock-like solidity of this flattened position, with the body spread – if not sprawled – as if for sacrifice, is the right thing to do. The whole world seems to clamour of its rightness in my inner ear. A voice, as if from nowhere, seems to call from the ceiling's height, acknowledging that I have done all that I need to do. There is no further for me to fall. I am as close to solid ground as I will ever need to be. I have testified, by this posture, that I am utterly helpless and waiting. I have utterly extended myself, which is as much as to say: take me, crush me, re-fashion me at your whim. I can do no more. And I therefore do no more.

CCXXXVII

Voices! Yet more voices! Would that there could be a pause! Impossible. It is as if life itself exists, and must always exist, in order to interrogate itself, ceaselessly. There is sleep, of course, the brief interruptions of sleep, those delicious, fleeting numbnesses – seconds, minutes, fragments of hours – when the mind slackens its grip, the limbs fall slack, and we lie, awkwardly tumbled as puppets. Then, moments later (or so it always seems), the eye blinks awake in the dark, and starts peering out for meaning, form, context, and it all begins again, the never ending questions: who, why, where, when. And it must always be so because there is so great a distance to travel, and, though old, I know, by my own overwhelming ignorance, that I have barely begun. I have considered blinding myself, believing that it might bring about a welcome supercession of labour. The reason for this, I find myself arguing to myself, is simple – and perhaps far too simple-minded. It is the eye, the peering eye, which I recognise to be the source of all inquietude. It never ceases to see. The self-mirroring eye, our chief tormentor, never ceases to pose its tireless round of questions. The ever open eye, even when dust-choked or suppurating, is forever striving to gulp down the world in all its unwieldy immensity. And behind the everything that there is always to be seen, there is that greater shadow-world of the unseen which hangs behind it, forever further beckoning.

CCXXXVIII

I lay my hand across the eyes, the eyes of this other, eternally still now. I close the eyes. That offers a measure of satisfaction. It is as if I have done what needed to be done by a man such as myself. I have said to the grieving few who knew him, who embraced him, gathered here beside this bed: by this simple gesture, I have flung wide for him the portals of death. Let him now walk comfortably on. Do not call out to him. Wish him good speed on his journey. They look at me then, and as they look, I see that they are looking beyond me, to the walking man on his new journey, and he is not hesitating. He is not turning to look back at them. He no longer hangs desperately suspended between here and there. He is full to the brim with the wholesome fullness of his new death. He is skipping. He has a certain freshness about him.

CCXXXIX

I say to myself: it is when you are asleep that you are most capable of alighting on yourself because it is then that you are most innocently off your guard.

CCXL

Death is standing behind me once again, whispering words which are just beyond earshot. It is on such idling afternoons as this one that he presents himself to me, perfectly at ease, and in complete denial of the fact that I have not recognised him once again.

CCXLI

If you ask me – and I know that you are never likely to ask me because you are always so disinclined to turn yourself in my direction – I would tell you once again that I do not know how to love the world, that the world seems to me not to be loveable. Every nook is so barren, every object so casually indifferent to its future fate. And I do not exclude myself. I am the least loveable component of this tangled situation. I challenge you to put this to me. I challenge you to stand forth in front of me, fists clenched, and to make such a remark as this one. You will not be able to do so because only I myself am capable of rising to that occasion.

<h3 style="text-align:center">CCXLII</h3>

They have all gone from me, all at once, as if on cue. And it was all so cleanly done. It is as if there is nothing now but smoke surrounding me, a dirty miasma clouding my eye, in which, not unsurprisingly, I am rejoicing in a timely fashion. What is more, all routes to me have been blocked or barred, all bridges detonated, all streams sucked dry by this fierce, parching wind, which exists, oh sweetest of purgatives, to show me no mercy. My name has been expunged from the book of records. At last, in full knowledge of the fact that all this has happened at last, I can breathe again, knowing that the need to suffer needlessly has been lifted from me. They have lost all scent of me, whether it be sweet or acrid, and I can freely attend to my own affairs once again without let or hindrance. Blessing high piled upon blessing then.

<h3 style="text-align:center">CCXLIII</h3>

Return here. Mark out these distances. Cleave to this finger post as if your life depended upon it. If you leave now, the world will surely leave with you. The shape of this hand, as it hangs in the air, promises hope of a kind. I see them, everywhere, such slogans as these. It is as if they have been smeared across my eye balls. Nevertheless, I do not fail to persist. I do not fail to resist such feeble blandishments. In short, there is no going back, for any part of me.

CCXLIV

The sea has scooped up, as if in a broad-spread hand, its violent residue, and thrown it all back, proving thereby its potency. I, promenading back and forth, am looking on in admiration, a little set apart from it all. You are there too, Paul, I see, crawling on all fours up the sea-sucked gravel, a helpless child again, with bloodied knees and bloodied hands, wailing at me, asking to be rescued. I am here to lecture you, to tell you of the sea and its backbone, the sea and its spumy flurries, the sea and its long, smooth curves of timeless satisfaction. When you have heaved yourself upright again, at such a future hour as that one, we can consider our friendship again. We can take stock.

CCXLV

It is these multiple acts of writing, heaping up here in front of me, one by one, which are causing me to flee away from myself. The more I write into and out of myself, the more distant I become. I stand now on this promontory beside the sea, looking back so far in the direction of the land that nothing and no one is any longer recognisable to me. It is these words which are dragging me down, deeper and deeper, into this process of estrangement. Which is, of course, profoundly amusing to me and perpetually enriching into the bargain because nothing is more tiresome than to be utterly familiar to yourself. Who would not wish to embrace the ever more engulfing darkness of the labyrinthine otherness of the self?

CCXLVI

It is your wife who is calling out to you, Paul. You are not listening to her. You have displaced yourself. You are attending to yourself alone, in that room where you sit, beneath the eaves, in Paris. It is such a small room, so pleasurably confining. Your wife raises a helpless hand to you. She is surely signalling to you across the distances. You become aware of a certain indefinable something in the air around you. You in your turn raise your head from your books. It is a long and heavy pull. It is the pull of the weight and the bulk of a boulder, raised from the depths of a well. You turn your head about, quizzical as a bird. You seem not to see her. There are these eddyings of air around your head. You wheel a little. They refresh you. You are smiling into new sunlight. You are giddily honing your pleasures. That distant signalling is fading and fading. She is removing herself from you. She is seeking out sources of contentment which must surely exclude you.

CCXLVII

To speak intermittently, here or elsewhere, and best of all here, in this laboratory of my interior life. To let the spaces between the words swell and then begin to rhapsodise as if they were so full of confidence, so world-commanding in their inexplicable muteness. It is these spaces that I must cleave to because they are infinitely extendable and utterly malleable. I work with them, I commune with them, minute by minute. I throw the finest of fine stones into the depths of them and listen out for all that they might wish to be telling me. What do I hear? And then, everywhere that I begin to look, whether here or elsewhere, there are spaces of a similar amplitude, of a similar unconfinedness, and nowhere better than between the stars, where I am staring now, measuring them by raising my hand and splaying out these fingers of mine, setting my finger's span against all that ungainsayable immensity.

CCXLVIII

Yes, there is always the I Am, albeit pencil-thin on a meagre day, a day as off-kilter as this one, in which I, standing here on this door step, do nothing but face into a chilling wind, though it is by no

means hectic or blustery. It has not striven to overawe me by outpacing itself. In that I Am resides the self's solidity, I tell myself, flexing the ever stiffening joints of the hand, as is customary. It is neither bulky nor immense, neither tall nor short. Everything is relative to everything else. There is no other means of making understanding happen. To establish reasonableness, habits of deportment, even a certain noble fixity of gaze, by standing, for minutes on end, beside the hollyhock (as I do now) in front of this window, that is my objective. That hollyhock knows, as if instinctively, how to respond to the wind's gentle cajolings, the wind's mighty cudgellings. There is a certain tact in its dealings with me. It notices how I walk down the steps, side on, allowing for my slight bodily infirmity. It hears how I clear the rattle from my throat, as if preparing to address it on matters of the moment. Meanwhile, it keeps a weather eye on that church which it must forever face. It knows to whom or to what it is finally accountable. I am tiptoeing towards it from behind, slightly apologetically. I am a witness to a little gentle swaying of the long, thin stem, which I describe to myself as anticipatory.

CCXLIX

Habits of speed. Habits of such dragging dilatoriness. Habits of brilliant clarity. And then there is this leadenness or deadness behind the eyes, as if a bar of metal has been inserted there with such violence; a deadening, a rifting so overwhelming that no part cleaves to any other part... Ah, how to second-guess what is to be shaped or conjured from all this perpetually heaving and shifting formlessness! It was surely a miracle, his life, how Paul made it happen, how he swam forward, day by day, cleaving the waves, without seeming interruption; or, considered in another way, how he shaped these blocks, constructed these outposts, built these mighty, reticulated walls from sequences of mere words, which surely began in so little. Being mere flesh and blood, he would surely have known that there is always so little to be had at rise of morning, so little to be found, so little to be heaved from the depths. So much confusion spins around the head when the body, undone by dark, is covered by a single blanket on a bed. It is as if all that giddy, headlong spinning must surely go on forever, everything falling and hurtling away from everything else... And yet, slowly, little by little, we rise, and, having tossed it off, something gradually comes to rest or perhaps to settle, a sediment of sorts, and it is always enough, always just enough, to enable us to continue along the way. But it is never more than this. This *this* of which I speak, somewhat awkwardly, is always on the brink of being too little. And, really, how much, in all actuality, is this *this*? Is it not as if I am striving, once again, to prove to myself that I can and must continue to be alive in this place, this miserable, confining space of a place, by shouting out this one word, and a word of such overwhelming insignificance, at the top of my voice?

CCL

Nothing is lost then. Nothing is lost forever. Everything must again foregather, in this place or some other. The particles are dancing once again, footing featly as they go. And when we descend the stairs, we find ourselves numbering them all over again, with a kind of idle jocularity: the plates, the cups, the sieve for straining off water. Bending over the sink once again, we see the water, water as it has always been, still streaming through the fingers. And we let it flow on, faster and faster, and even splash up into the face, a freshening assault of cold water. A face come alive with water, a face streaming with chains, droplets, necklaces of water, such a face is alive with new beginnings. It is not a face without hope. Mine is not a face without hope.

CCLI

It is how it must be, always. There is a need to return to each flaw, each mistake, each misdemeanour. They are never not present to me, on this day and any other, fierily alive within me, burning bright. I am staggering across this darkened room, dizzy, reeling, and nursing a glancing blow to the side of the head. Its source feels unknowable. Did I strike? Or was I struck? I may have turned my body too quickly and engaged with the rough bricks of the kitchen wall, like some dolt going through his drunken capers with a besotted strip of a girl at a village fete. And yet it is the wall which struck me, I feel that deep within me as I touch at the wound again oh so tenderly. The wall, surely, was my aggressor, and it struck me in punishment. It knew – as walls must always know – that this blow to the cheek was exactly what I was required to suffer. Or put it like this. She had spoken to me when my back was turned. I had not heeded her words. I was not listening. I had not responded. I was inhabiting dream worlds of my own conjuring. Grabbing hold of my shoulder, she had spun me round like a child's top, and then her fist had engaged with my face, tenderising the cheek of the small child which I then had been. I am standing in front of her again now, in the utmost bewilderment, seeing it all happen, being that child again. I cannot muster the words. Tears, hot, copious tears, have blinded my eyes. All the words have fled from me.

CCLII

I cup it, closing my eyes. I let it diffuse its consoling mysteries... Yes, the steadying, grounding, soothing, world-pardoning warmth of the coffee in this bowl, when I sit prayerfully at this kitchen table and raise it once again to my lips, when I feel its wash against my underlip like the lapping of a warm summer sea, is the day's climacteric. And, as if to add forgiveness to soothingness, the sunlight has now splashed itself across my hands, reassuring me that all is well again, and as if to cajole me into believing that the silence of this morning will never be interrupted or snuffed out by some brutish interloper juddering the very frame of the door with his fist. I am hunched over this bowl, and over the bread on my plate too. As I stare down at it, a touch dreamily, the bread seems to mutter its customary words of reassurance back to me. *Si on a le pain, on est sauvé*, it is saying to me, again and again, words as lulling as any sacred litany on this warmest of spring mornings. And I nod back at it in my turn because I know this to be true, now and forever, that this daily bread, this fresh-baked, plumped out, rough stick of bread, is my prop, my solace and the hope of my salvation. This bread, when I masticate it, so slowly, bears me onward towards the light, and when I tear off chunks of it, again and again, I inwardly suffer the tearing of His own dear flesh for my sake. And when I swallow it down, I even become Him, just a little. Perhaps even a little more than I deserve.

CCLIII

I can summarise it quite neatly, quite crisply, if you insist upon it, and I see that you do – perhaps for the sake of clarity. You had asked me to accompany you to the edge of the stream, and then beyond. You had pointed in the general direction of that beyond, and I had understood you. Was it quite so clear cut though? Is it not in fact true that only some part of you was asking, some part of you beckoning? Granted, it was not a request formed of so many words. It was perhaps in the way that your body had been shifting from side to side, and even gently swaying a little, as you swept the *carrelage* with the broom. That degree of stealth. Your back was turned to me. I was idling at the kitchen table, preparing myself to ascend the stairs to the upper room and back to the familiar, beloved company of my writing desk and my books and my bed. I had delayed for a little too long. It was uncustomary for me to be

standing in that room with you for so long. Time must have been stretching. I had been looking for something. Perhaps at the hour of your arrival – and you had arrived just minutes before – I had been busy searching for myself. Had these two things coincided by accident, the fact of your being there, albeit briefly, in my company, and my daily, ceaseless search for a final answer, an answer that will satisfy me forever? I knew, of course, that there was no such answer. I knew that I had been fooling only myself by dallying with such a proposition. Nevertheless, if was then that you spoke to me, though not in so many words. It was then that I knew you had invited me to accompany you, though not on this particular morning, and not with a gesture of the hand. For all that, the message could not have been clearer: there would be a moment much more opportune than this one, and it would surely be our moment. And it would come soon enough, and it would descend like a lightning bolt.

CCLIV

I have no strength to face the new day. I have no strength to fight back against its oncoming presence. I have no strength to describe or to resist – far better to resist than to describe, I know this for a fact – the power of the sun's rays as they sweep across my face, as if wishing to familiarise themselves with a thing of great fascination because so long occluded or estranged. Had I the strength to raise my hand, I might peel off the rays of the sun, one by one, and leave myself in the dark again. I know myself to be incapable of such a thing. I know myself to be entirely at the mercy of that which must, every new day, supervene. I am being dragged, feet-first, through the mud of my life, and I am helpless to resist. And then, just then, the clock strikes on the hour, as if beckoning me to some new awakening. And some part of me – just enough, it has to be said – finds itself responding with a yelp of new found joy, snatched from goodness knows where in the universe. I throw off the covers. I discover myself yet again.

CCLV

You are the nightlight, a small thing hovering close by, small and fleeting as a firefly in the eerie dark of the garden. When I go to catch at you, you are no longer there in front of me. You have already eluded me. I imagine to myself that I may have imagined you after all. Or perhaps you are not the nightlight at all but the daylight, and there is so much of you, you surround me and engulf me so comprehensively, that I am forced to hang back once again and admit defeat. There is always too much of you. You blind me with your presence here. You are coming at me from all directions, bearing down upon me from all sides. I both yearn for you and desperately fear you. When you arrive – and surely it will not be long – a new clarity of purpose will become evident to me. I will be illuminated by the light of you. The light of the self, forever sputtering, will once again count for nothing, and I will be at peace. I call those two the twin possibilities, and I visit them regularly.

CCLVI

Little by little it is happening. I cannot deny that I am feeling it happening. The earth is softening and yielding beneath my feet. The boards of the kitchen floor have parted like the twin curtains of some theatre, and I am staring down into the softened earth where I must walk, where it will be forever incumbent upon me to walk. And as I do so, the weight of me, such as it is – it is more than enough – causes my feet and my legs to be swallowed up inch by inch. I smell and I feel the uneven mud of the ground, in all its cloggy reek, rising, slowly rising, up and up, as far as the level of my chin. And I know that soon enough I will be required to eat of that earth, mouthful by ever more constricting mouthful, until I can do no more, until I must surely choke and gag upon it. I feel my jaws and my teeth, such ones as remain to me, working with a terrible, onward regularity, like the weary clanking of the trusting pistons of some bygone machine stranded in a field. I cannot make myself pause. I cannot make myself stop. And soon enough this earth at my feet, this earth which has been greedily engulfing my feet, will swallow me up in my entirety, and I will lie there, prone, like the earth itself, hugely swelled and vacant of eye. I will be nothing but earth then, and there will be for me no other fact to reflect upon throughout all eternity, nothing but this cloggy, clotted earthiness from which I must surely be compounded and composed forever. Or, if not this, what, I earnestly find myself asking you?

CCLVII

It was a day like no other. I found myself reading his words, one by one, as I hovered at his shoulder and watched him writing them down in that sloping hand of his. Then, having listened so carefully to his slow delivery, I repeated them after him, trying my best to mimic, syllable by syllable, his orotundity. Did I fall far short? I tried to sculpt his words in the air so that they could be seen, bright- shining in the darkness of that room. It was my hope, if not my reckless belief, that he would turn, all of a sudden, in his chair, to face me, and then slowly admire, the astonishing miracle of the physical embodiment of this uncannily seductive echo at his back. But he did not do so. He heard only himself, such was the degree of his self-absorption. He was quite deaf to me. And I cared so little that I wept for joy, and even found myself saying out loud, to the rafters and the chair and the stub of my bedside candle: see just how mistaken he is, see how his mind is working, see how he honestly believes that these words that he is writing and uttering are his alone. None of this is true, of course. By the sharing of them with me in this way, he has made us co-creators of his mysteries! And the chair on which he was sitting, the table top upon which his elbows rested, my stub of candle which overlooked him, and even the dust motes hovering in the air above his head, they all believed me. And I praised myself for this near overwhelming seizure of self-confidence.

CCLVIII

Once again I am waiting here for so little to happen. It comes on, again and again and again. My life is a scrap of paper, tossed by the wind.

CCLIX

Let me consider my hand again as it lies here upon this table top, how it has commanded, commended, dissuaded, deceived. Let me consider its disproportionate effectiveness as a tool of persuasion. I see it resting here now, as if its labours were over. And yet they are never over. The mind calls it to arms again, daily, hourly, and it rises up, ready, attentive, quick to do its bidding.

CCLX

I am wholly in the grip of this obsession with the idea of the Supreme Being, his loftiness, his otherness, his grandiosity, his comprehensiveness. And yet I myself am too small and too weak and too timid even to conceive of him. Who then placed this idol in front of me? Who taunted me with the idea of his existence? And who will have the strength to snatch him away again?

CCLXI

My disgust with literature amounts to a horror of fabrication and freakish puerility. That which is made can so easily be unmade. Are we not encouraging each other to think like those children who are forever diverted by the deft tumbling of coloured balls? The reality of all this invention is so mild-mannered, so specious.

CCLXII

To think – as I do now – is to raise oneself above the mundane cruelties of this makeshift world. It is at such moments as these that I rise above myself. And, needless to say, I rise above you.

CCLXIII

If I could keep up with the pulsing of my heart, I would be running. In fact, I am sleeping, and the world (in so far as it knows me at all) is passing me by on the other side. How fortunate I am to be subject to such forces of inertia.

CCLXIV

I have said this to myself repeatedly in order all the better to convince myself of the truth of my own words. I have profited by my loneliness. I have inserted myself into the narrowest interstices of my own life.

CCLXV

Is it the future of which I am now catching a glimpse through this window? There are flurryings and buffetings out there. My poor trees are being whip-lashed, mercilessly. Which can mean one thing only: it is all, once again, upon the point of departure. By which I mean the whole of my life because all this must surely be a portent. Is it all now threatening to leave without me? Nothing is safe here, within or without. Who can sort the one from the other? Nothing lives with me here in this house in a state of contentment, whether it be object or person. Nothing is nailed to solid ground. It all disperses, it all must surely slip away as readily as night follows day. The wind sees to that, blowing hither and thither without forethought or conscience. What must I then do today to settle myself, to calm my many rancorous voices, to still these limbs of mine, which refuse to stay still even when I am seated? My knees bounce and bounce beneath this desk, dislodging books and papers. If I could only embrace the stillness of death, all would surely be well with me. Liar, I say to myself. There is no knowing what happens to us after death. There is merely this appetite, this craving for the illusory solace of non-being, which rears up again on a blank and unseasonable day such as this one.

CCLXVI

It is time now for a little gentle mockery at the expense of my protector. Who invested this house with such outlandish airs and graces? Who blessed this poor, four-square thing, set down on the edge of a field, with such a prideful measure of self-preening? Who gifted it with this Grecian pediment? Who promised it a grand *Porte Cochère* directly beneath, and then snatched that promise away again? Who reared up these windows, only to have them give onto the lumpen majesty of a church which has, in all its many centuries, never brooked a rival? Who, in short, has such pretence as this place? I have. I alone am perhaps its equal. I too strut and preen and posture. From it I have learnt such habits. Which of the two of us then is the more blameworthy?

CCLXVII

There is no better way than to stand alone. There is no better way than to be answerable to no one. I ask myself only such questions as I am able to answer. I set my own boundaries. I never exceed the possibilities of my own life. I am beholden to no one. No one bests me. No one challenges or beats me. No one wrong-foots me. My ears are deaf to the clamorous voices of hatred. I move serenely forward, neither looking to left nor to right. I lift up each foot one by one, first the left and then the right, with the utmost care. Do you yourself possess so many reasons to be roundly pitied?

CCLXVIII

I wished him god speed, and he was gone from me within a moment. I looked everywhere for traces of his presence, physical or otherwise. I listened out for the notes of his voice, the head-notes, small-scale, furtive trillings of the kind that any small bird might make. I cocked an ear for his footfalls, steady, lovely, regular, akin to my own. I was possessed by this overwhelming passion to have him still with me, but he was gone from me, within a moment, leaving no trace of himself. At which point I grew angry, cursing myself.

CCLXIX

Of nothing I came, and to nothing I shall return. It is that which happens between the two conditions, the years of uncertainty, the furtive anxieties, the headlong bolts of unreasonable confidence... I am a circus act, wheeling high in the air as the crowd gapes and gasps. I am a lowly, creeping thing, possessed of only sufficient self-knowledge to creep along a little further. I boom from my battlements. I squeak and I mew and I pine from my hole in this casement. What is there hereabouts that is able to tell me what shall become of me?

CCLXX

I heard him leave the house this morning. I experienced that customary twinge of regret to see him go. He always slips out so easily, as if his departure is the satisfactory drawing to the close of a chapter in the history of our lives together, no matter how brief. I could tell from his gait that he was satisfied with his words, that he

was abreast of himself. There was no sense of that desperate,endless seeking out such as I myself experience, daily. He had laboured. He had conquered. I watched him carefully as he retreated from me, the smooth-glidingness of his body. I examined the angle of his head. I found myself admiring once again the pursing of his lips, and what that told me about the solidity of his character. I found myself yearning to emulate that way he has of facing into the morning sun, as if challenging it to do its worst. There is such an enviable degree of complicity between Paul and the sun. They are as twin brothers, linking arms, heads leaning together, whispering conspiratorially. Paul does not fear its influence upon him. He does not fear the way in which the sun always seeks us out again, peering into every corner of our lives, the least cranny of our being, soundlessly alighting upon the edge of the pillow at dawn with its first words of warning. He has the strength of character to fight back against the undeniable fact that the sun is our searing conscience. There is nothing I fear more than the eye of the sun.

CCLXXI

I stood perfectly still, arms akimbo, eyes tight shut. My very breathing, it seemed to me just then, was in a state of heightened suspension. I was serenely alone at last, wholly self-reliant, entirely self-dependable, set fast and wholly grounded within the kingdom of myself. Above all else, I was no longer falling. The fear of that endless, headlong falling, down, down through the ever thickening darkness, had left me. It had been whisked away, as if by some act of prestidigitation. Yes, occasionally, as now, it does leave me, and for such brief interruptions in this life of endless falling, I never fail to give heartfelt thanks. I even opened my eyes, and saw to my amazement how everything had come to rest about me, by way of encouragement. There was no shifting of any kind, no gentle juddering, no stirring from any corner. Even the wind had ceased to breathe through the cracks in the rotten surrounds of the window. Everything about me, my entire immediate known world, possessed the solidity, the indomitability of stone. Never to be budged. Never to be shaken to its foundations. Never to be overthrown. To stare ahead liked this, unmoving, pinioned and secure in one's being, and to know nothing but this security. I kneeled then. I bent over and kissed the very boards of the floor. I tasted, I even welcomed, the dust.

CCLXXII

To describe oneself – or to be described by some other – as this sentient being called man is wholly insufficient, the merest of beginnings. It is simply not adequate to life's multiple occasions. It tells us so little. It is so costive. It holds out no promises, no gifts, no sweet expectations of any kind. And so it is incumbent upon us to build on this little by striving to uncover and cultivate such talents as we are able to discover deep within us, having delved and delved. Alas, to seek is not to find. I have found so little. I consist, in sum, of the capacity to chastise, to warn, to fulminate against the world. Could these be described as positive or health-giving attributes at all? Humorous jester. And yet, finally, this is what I find that I amount to. I am a being who exists to deny the world and all its pleasures, to make little of life in all its abundance, to strip that abundance away, to rob the colours from the flowers, to frown at the frivolities of every passing hour. To point to death alone as life's chastening pill. May the world pity me.

CCLXXIII

Let me make this confession at last. I have withheld the truth of things from you for far too long. I have been making light of these labours of mine at this desk, in front of this window, confronting the stony and unbudgeable reality of this church, to which my body

and my soul have pledged allegiance. The fact is that I am living within these pages, these testamentary fragments. In fact, it is here alone that I could be said to be alive at all. There is nothing for me – and nothing of me – beyond the confines of these flimsy sheets of paper. Otherwise, life consists of its multiple daily blanknesses. I squeeze and I squeeze it like a lemon in the fist, but it yields up to me so little. In short, I must confess to you now that I am nothing and no one other than what I am telling you here, and to make this confession to you in this way, covertly, is to give my life its sole, tiny spark of ignition.

CCLXXIV

It was not so easily said, what I have just confessed to you. In fact, what I have just told you is tantamount to a declaration that I have been lying to you all this time. I began – when exactly was it that I began? – by speaking of random verbal outpourings to which I was paying far too little attention. My efforts, unlike the writings of Paul, were tentative, clumsy, brutish, short and inconsequential. They had no life to them. They dragged their weary way from sentence to sentence. And I was helpless to do anything other than what I was doing precisely because I was wholly at the mercy of my own blundering clumsiness. I lacked the capacity – the intellect, the searing insights, the skills – to endow my words with life, to breathe life into them as life had once been breathed into me. I gave each one a number – one, two, three and on – because that method of organisation seemed simple and unpretentious. It was a way of doing nothing other than separate one gobbet from another, no more and no less than that. As it happens, it was not quite that random. Calculation was being brought into play. The fact is that beneath and behind all this seeming nonchalance, I was all along striving and striving to do my best, honing and refining and polishing my every word, doing my utmost to bring something to perfection. Perhaps even to bring myself to perfection because was

I not after all seeking to give some meaning and some regularity to the dully disappointing to-ings and fro-ings of my life by ordering these fragments in this way? Was I not even setting myself up as a rival to Paul, as someone who would at first emulate him and then perhaps surpass him? Could that be what was driving me on, not an abiding love for this man, but a part-hidden desire to destroy by surpassing him?

CCLXXV

There has descended upon me a measure of calmness, and perhaps even a measure of self-possession. I have been soothed somewhat by listening to the flow of my own words. I now feel that there is space around me, that my own physical space, both within and without me, has expanded to accommodate a new breadth of thinking. Put simply, I now feel that I can breathe a little more easily. What is more, the words themselves are moving along a little faster. They are also gaining in confidence. Their footfall is more sure. I am seeing, as it were, a light ahead of me, a beckoning light. What it all amounts to is this, of which I am now increasingly convinced: I have half done with my labours. In short, I now know that in time there will be an end to all of this. I can even begin to foresee the time when I will fall silent, and it will be a silence of satisfied completion. I will hang my head on that day not too far ahead, and I will say to myself: at last it is over. Until now I have been moving, with great difficulty, through what has always felt to me like an ever thickening obscurity. I have been sorting nothing from nothing. This is no longer the case. My goal now seems less remote to me. I am less of the creeping blind man than I used to be. I have found - no, I am finding, let us not run before we can walk - the capacity to grasp hold of myself and to lead myself forward by the hand.

<h1 style="text-align:center">CCLXXVI</h1>

All of which conspires together to make for the greatest of difficulties, of course, because with this new found confidence comes a new found realisation that, as I have already declared, I am also lying to myself even as I begin, with such solemn, booming confidence, to speak of the truth. Why so? Because to accept that there is this way ahead is to exclude all other ways, to deny all the minor turns off this straight and narrow path, to set the eyes rigidly facing forward towards that which lies ahead, unswervingly. In short, to speak in this way is to obscure the fact that there is more than one way of describing this path to the truth, more than one credible bearer of the message, and more than one destination that is beckoning me towards it.

<h1 style="text-align:center">CCLXXVII</h1>

And so I have declared myself to be fully alive within the pages of this book. In fact, this monument made of words is the essence of my life, the better part of me. These words are laid down one beside another, in pleasing sequences (or so I flatter myself), rather in the way that one stone is laid beside another to create a path towards that singular destination of one's own desiring.

<h1 style="text-align:center">CCLXXVIII</h1>

A word is a hallowed thing. A word is also a sullied thing. It lives on the lips of men who pay it little attention and show it less respect. It is for this reason that certain words, and words laid down in certain combinations, are necessarily set apart, incubated in the minds of certain gifted men. Paul's words, for example. When I think of such matters, I call to kind most often his haunting locutions. When I stare at them, I stare into them. I disappear inside them. I lose myself in a cloud of excitable reverie. I know no way to extricate myself. I have no wish to extricate myself. I must call it poetry.

CCLXXIX

In declaring as little as I have declared, I am declaring much. It is as much as needs to be said. In fact, it is that which was urging to be said. Nothing counts for more than this. Besides all this, there are also the trivial, fleeting, back-and-forth washings of the everyday. They seldom impinge upon me. They are never what I would wish to retain. They are the smallest and most contemptible segments of the known world.

CCLXXX

The pleasure that I take in these words of mine is due to their strange opacity. You can never see through them to the half-formulated thoughts, the nail-biting hesitations, the tentative, provisional speculations that helped to bring them into being. In short, and in spite of the fact that I am always busy defending the truth of them for your delectation and bemusement, I must always prove, finally, to be wholly unknown to you, as these words are to me. Yet, let them sing in my stead.

CCLXXXI

These words are as a house to me. In fact, they are the very house in which I live here, as the priest of this village, knowing nothing other than this reality, which has whirled about my head for decades almost without number. At least, that is how it seems to me. The two, my words, as I choose to set them down here, in uneven row upon row, and this house in which I live, rooted and pinioned to its place in common with any other animal of fixed habitat, have become indistinguishable to me. But a house is something wholly other, you would surely try to persuade me. Not quite so. It is all a matter of deep-down-delving. A house is what you make of it, it is what you choose to fabricate from the idea of a place such as this one. And by this I am not referring to the crude fabric of this house, the materials from which it has been fashioned. I mean the idea of it as the shell in which I live, protected, defined and even somewhat aggrandised by its contours. And every day it is necessarily a little different because every day I find myself – I happen upon myself, let us say, with a modicum of surprise – choosing to define it anew. All is new born to me. The fall of light hereabouts is a great helpmate. Nothing is ever quite the same – the nature and the quality of my looking, the nature and the quality of that which there is to be seen... Take these spiders' webs, for example, and the way they hang pendent in the corners of this window. By a certain low, grey light they are wholly unseeable, unnoticeable, of no importance to me whatsoever. They fail, at such times as these, to part-define the nature of my being. I am alive here, perfectly, even smugly self-sufficient, without their defining presence inside me. And then on a wholly different morning – one of blaring, declamatory light, for example – I sit here amazed by their nature, the fact that something so small and so thin and so fragile, with its delicate, catherine-wheel-like, concentric wheelings, has been brought, on this morning as on no other, to such a state of perfection, and surely for my instant delectation. It is at such a moment as this that these webs seem to exist here in order to define the very world in which I live, by the way in which they hang here, gently stirring from time to time, in all their sweet, near heart-stopping fragility. And am I not, surely, such another? Yet not half so precious, with my reeking breath and these rackety skeletal fingers.

CCLXXXII

Let us speak of practicalities for a moment then. Let us strive to distract ourselves from these higher matters. The way in which I make my words – by which I mean fashion my own handwriting – is vexing me more and more. As my eyesight, little by little, begins to fail, it becomes more and more incumbent upon me to increase the size of my letters and my words in order to improve the legibility of my writing. Put simply, if I cannot see, I am incapable of knowing what it is that I have written. The thoughts themselves – let us call them that for want of better – are always so fleeting, so elusive. They come and they go, quick and darting as fireflies. One flares in front of me, almost dazzling my sight. The heart thumps in excited recognition. And then it is gone, and I am left, dumbstruck, and looking after it wonderingly, because already I have forgotten the very words that I happened to pluck, in an instant of illumination, out of the air. And so I strive to slow down the nature of my thinking, and also, simultaneously, to increase the size of my words and even the spaces between the words. Yet even as I try to do this, some dark vixen of a countervailing impulse is urging me in quite the opposite direction, and I find that my words, because part of me is desperately striving to do the contrary, are decreasing in size because in their heart of hearts they do not really want to be seen. They are enjoying their will-o'-the-wispish half-hiddenness. They want above all to be playing hide and seek through the hedgerows. They enjoy nothing better than coaxing from me these heavy, desk-top thumps of sheer exasperation.

CCLXXXIII

I am trying to demand less of my life, that is the truth of it. I have no further wish to be running so hard in this futile race to the finish. I see no competitors at my side. I am not in the business of exchanging anxious glances. I am not biting down on my bloodless lips. My heart is not racing in anticipation. There is no one hereabouts to encourage me on. And even if I were to win, there would be no one here to embrace me. Why is it then that each new morning a heavy bell seems to toll once again inside this glooming belfry of my head, and I drag myself upright, believing that I am once again being called to account for myself? Why is it that I pick up this pen once again and then watch myself labouring to give birth to yet more foolish remarks, cursory and provisional as ever, in some vain hope that in the opinion of you and you and you, I will have adequately accounted for whatever it is that I have been doing here, long hour after long hour? How do I possess the strength yet again to read my own words? And how is it that I still retain the perversity to believe them to be, in spite of all warnings from myself to the contrary, diverting?

CCLXXXIV

Is it easier to define the self by considering the nature of one's shadow? Or not? It looms. And then it looms. From time to time, it appears to speaks to me inwardly without the need for words. It beckons me on by walking in step with me. We go together, tentatively, or as the case may be. It trails along behind, sullenly. It is forever faithful as only it knows how to be. It is my faintest of faint echoings. And yet it is also crude and defiant. (Can I call that which does not respond to me defiant?) A shadow thrown down at one's feet is a featureless no thing of a thing, an embodiment of crisp outline and muddy interior, a mass of unrelieved darkness which appears to swim and to swim. Which means that I cannot see it in the round. It does not exist in front of me in readiness to return stare for stare. I cannot pose questions of if because it does not possess the quickening density of being. In short, my shadow is never amiable. It is not a friend to me. It has never given back to me like for like when I have spoken. And yet it never hesitates to judge me, and I never cease to experience pain and embarrassment in its presence.

CCLXXXV

I raise up now, for want of better, on a cheerful day of unrestrained bluster, this window space behind my desk, through which the light first inveigles itself, and then splashes down upon me when it so chooses. I rise up from my chair as if beckoned by some eager interlocutor. Yet there is no one here. Only my window waits for me. I push away my desk slightly to make space for myself, and then I ease myself up onto its ledge, that generously proportioned, shelf-like space. Leaning in as I twist and push forward the mass of my rather unwilling body, I extend my two hands up, up into its farthest corners. I touch, quite delicately, the crumbling, paint-thirsty rottenness of the wood. Settled there now, I observe how the glass dimples and gives back to me, quite cheerily readily, a morning light which cannot exactly be the true light. It is a light mediated by so much dust and age-old grime, and so be it. I stare now, and once again I stare, penned and small here as I am, framed by this window, across the roof tops, which I appraise now, beyond and then far below me, as they fall away from me down the valley, in their many uneven angles, the terracotta gleam of them. Below them are outbuildings, pasture land and the careful patterning of fields of rucked soil. Any idle animal, human or otherwise, could observe me up here, observing. I could be the easy victim of any idling eye as I look down from here at the world from my very particular vantage point. And this is such a boundlessly pleasurable place to be because it seems to contain me and confine me and define my shape so well, not only the physical fact of me but also the idea of me, boxed in here so tidily like a well wrapped gift, and I feel this more and more as I continue to squeeze my bonily cumbersome sprawlingness into its narrow confines. It contains me now, almost wholly, and this neat containment appears to have lent, when I record all this hours later, a certain quickening and sharpening to my words. The shape of the embrasure itself has imposed a new clarity upon me. By seeing through this window from this space, I seem also to be seeing through and deep into the eye that observes these things, by which I mean my own eye, of course, first filling me to the brim with the clarity of its light and then shaping me, trimming me, bodily, as a tailor, slack measuring tape in teeth, might tap me down with his hands as he sizes me up for my garments. Yes, I am so happy here in this window space, trapped in this moment between all other moments. My spirit, fully awake, and wholly embodied now, is almost prepared to launch itself from this space. It lacks the foolhardiness to do so, needless to say.

CCLXXXVI

What do I know exactly when I am said to know what I know? The door in front of me is closed. And yet it is not closed because at that very moment, the moment at which I approach it, it opens up readily for another man who has just stepped up in front of me. He both resembles me and does not resemble me. We are of a similar height, I see. We also possess a similar gait. And yet now he is walking with an ever quickening step – I am seeing him still, beyond the door now, on the other side, readily and rapidly conversing with other men of his acquaintance – I know that they are acquainted by the ease with which they exchange volleys of pleasantries – and generally behaving with an ease and a casual confidence of which I am wholly incapable. As he raises his glass to another, he turns to face me, and we lock glances. It is indeed myself that I am staring at, so bemusedly, and yet here I still stand, on the wrong side of the door, in full possession, still, of my many unanswered questions about what exactly it is that I know when I am said to know what I know.

Let me make it plain to you. It was a nightmare in all but name, and yet it did not happen during the long hours of the night, those hours when the worst always battens down upon me, and yanks me, helpless, hither and thither, until I am a ragged, sweat-soaked, trembling less-than-nothing of a man. No, it was at a high moment of sweetest daylight, when the very air seemed to be singing at the opened door, and my chin was raised and mouth ajar as if about to suck in some liquid delectation that was already pouring down through the upper air... Yes, it was then that it happened. An image, winging down at lightning speed as if from nowhere, transfixed me, an image of a great scroll of words, streaming down from the top of my desk upstairs, down onto the floor, an unfurling scroll which appeared to be alive in all but name as it struggled to writhe away from me even as I did my best to trap it in its headlong flight with my hands, and even stamp down upon it with my foot. That great scroll of my words, even as I watched in horror and dismay, was stealing away from me, and not that only. It was worse than that by far. The words I had written, all those thousand upon thousand of words over which I had laboured, and which you are currently reading with such dutifulness, it is as if they were dissolving like liquid down the page. I would look at a single line and observe how the sturdy uprights of those letters I had deployed appeared now to be writhing, bending about, and even wilting down to the horizontal. My words were falling. My words were collapsing in on themselves. My words were giving up the ghost in front of me. My words lacked the courage of their own convictions. It was as if nothing I had ever written could possibly survive because it simply did not deserve to survive. My words had been judged to be wanting.

For days after, I was capable of nothing at all. I did not eat. I did not drink. I did not even moisten the edges of my lips with water from the sink. When I rose up from my bed at all – seldom – it was as if a bewildered ghost was drifting from side to side, seeking to understand for what reason it had to suffer such a state of bodilessness, and, needless to say, receiving no answer in response. Everything that I saw through my eyes had thinned and paled and receded a goodly distance from me. The world before me had been robbed of all colour, all substance. No one and nothing was vivid to me, and I was not vivid to myself. I was helplessly adrift at the outer margins. It was during these hours that I began to remove all the books from my desk. Someone other than myself seemed to be urging me to do so. I arranged them in towering, teetering, ziggurat-like heaps across the floor, and then I slowly made my way between them, twisting and turning about ritualistically. Back and forth I went, for hours at a time. I lost track of all notion of time. I had stepped outside time. The strangest fact of all was that there were no words in my head, merely a thick misty clotting which had descended upon me like a veil, so thick that it seemed to be the visual embodiment of a profound deafness, that state of which I have such a horror. Days, weeks – who knows how long? – seemed to pass me by, and then one morning, I awoke to find myself idly rolling the stub of a favourite pencil between thumb and finger, and when, curious, I raised it to my eye, I experienced this strange urging. Write, it seemed to be saying to me, in spite of all that has gone before, write, begin again. And I stood up then, and I dressed myself, and I ate, and I wrote. I had begun again.

CCLXXXIX

I have anatomised the light, as I have often been urged to do by my reading. The words have risen up in front of me, as if leaping off the page in their headlong urgency: look into the light, see into the light, unflinching. I have not only heeded. I have gone further. I have walked into the light, steadily, and with purpose. I have not been unnerved by its bright-shiningness. I have needed no protection.

CCXC

Each sentence moves steadily ahead of me, seeking out its goal, asking similar questions. My hand drives these words of mine along, and yet it also seems to follow after, as if the words themselves, even as they emerge as if by some miracle in front of me, are dictating the direction in which they chance to move. There is such a pentness, such an excitement within me. Fires burn inside me, small, fierce, compacted fires, quick-spurting, and larger ones too, which almost rise up and engulf my face, such is their unruly ferocity. They burn off the skin, they devour the features of my face so comprehensively that when I come to examine the state of myself in the mirror minutes later, I see nothing but a black, amorphous stub of a head, as if fresh charred by damnable weapons of war. I begin then, with the utmost delicacy, the task of re-finding myself again, the features I faintly remembered from yesterday, that look of mine, so habitual, when I appraise the bowed head of a supplicant at the altar, which seems to say: be raised up now, child, let all your burdens fall away from you. I am calmed then by the sight of myself re-emerging. Little by little I am beginning to recognise myself as I am, as I have always been. And then, quite quietly, quite calmly, and with resolute step, I return to my desk in order to continue with my investigations. Touching pen to paper, and holding my breath, I encourage the next bold act of errancy.

CCXCI

The rich colour of this local wine, my favourite, is not exactly the red of my blood. It is not then myself that I quaff, when I drink down this bottle to the dregs on any fragile evening of slowpleasingness, slowly, sip by soothing sip. Not necessarily. I recognise the glories of it. The world into which it admits me, yawning so expansively, appears to expand inside me, working its way with me, coaxingly, like a lover. And when I present it to the table, I carry it in my cupped hands as if it were a lover to be discovered, enfolding the bottle's swelling shapeliness in this unsullied white linen napkin within my own two cupped hands, as if I am gently grasping the waist of a phantom lover. And then, slowly, having let slip the linen to the table, I ease the bottle over, and I pour, with a quite fastidious slowness, letting the glass fill to a certain point and no more. There is grossness in a brimming glass. This is my slow dreaming hour, when I let slip the shackles of duty and conscience. I pick up books, one by one, from my desk, and I let my eyes swim amongst words without fully comprehending them. I bounce around amongst my words, and images, in their multitudes, rise up unbidden. I am not exactly sleeping until I am properly sleeping.

CCXCII

I am bounded, shaped, defined by this track to the door, across a light crepitation of gravel, this track which willingly transports me from garden gate to the short, steep flight of stone steps which ascend to the side door of the house, so often sun-blessed when flung back to take in the expansiveness of new morning. I move, repeatedly, across my own footprints (in so far as I am able to see them at all), matching new steps to old, endeavouring to ensure that all remains the same, always. It is a form of security which I am seeking in this daily (hourly, if need be) replication of my own

regular pattern of movements. It is to say to myself: this is the man you once were, and that you will always be. I even try to remind myself of what exactly I was thinking when I last took these few steps – there are nine of them in all, I have counted them exhaustively – from gate to door, and then perhaps even back again. I interrogate the nodding heads of the hollyhocks or the squat shapes of the lavender bushes at the level of my calf. I brush against them, always, and quite deliberately, when I pass them by, because I want the sweet smell of lavender to adhere to the hem of my *soutane*. It is this that I would wish for most of all, that the lavender will cling to me, unseen and yet forever present. When I come to fold that garment upon itself later, and lay it aside on the chair next to my bed, I will first sniff that smell again. I will lift it, somewhat reverentially, to my nose, and I will experience, for myself alone, a small and fleeting paradise of sorts in its sweet, narcotising aroma.

CCXCIII

Nothing is ever quite at rest in this miserable, ghostly house about which I seem to be forever racketing, for all its seeming smallness. Mice scurry. My thoughts scurry on after. A gentle breeze lifts a corner of the sheet upon which I am writing these words, and it does not listen – it never listens – when I command it to stay still. I am not a miracle maker. I cannot order the world to be at rest. And this is in the nature of things. There is a restlessness everywhere, now and forever more. It is always so headlong, so pell mell. The stars wheel, the clouds race, a man idles across a field to attend to a cow with its hind parts stuck in a bog. Nothing ever has the time or the patience to reflect upon itself. There is never any cessation. The world's mouth will not be stoppered. There will always be this howling, this braying, this ceaseless, ear-assaulting caterwauling. Even my own body is not immune to this disease of ceaseless stirring. A knee must shift about in the bed, as if in some great hurry to be gone from here or there or anywhere. And yet it does not go, ever, because the body is asleep. And yet some part of this same body must surely be saying: we must be moving onward! Why so? Because in the opinion of the body, to remain utterly still is to be dead to life's ceaseless pulsings. Is to stand, stare and reflect then tantamount to dying? Must I die when I lie here and close my eyes? Can I not be accorded the grace to stay still?

CCXCIV

The world has fallen in again, and it has happened, all of a sudden. There was quietude in here until just moments ago, the fixed quietude of new morning, and then there was this... A man's shrilling whistle from a field – is he calling to some animal? – has pinned me to the door. And now I am spinning, helpless, like a Catherine wheel. There is a riot inside this head of mine. Furniture is being heaved about, feet engage with faces, bodies are slumped over, inert as sacks. I clap my hands to my ears. I pace back and forth. I sing a favourite aria to myself, as loudly as I am able. I stuff wads of paper into my ears. Nothing succeeds. The drilling of noise, noise continues. I think of St Sebastian. I imagine his arrow wounds, and of how he once suffered so, slumped forward, that magnificent young body. One by one I remove those arrows from his flesh, and as I do so, as if by some miracle, the whistling recedes, little by little, to the smallest, least painful of pin pricks, and then it vanishes. The world of my body recomposes itself. This house shrinks back to its proper proportions. Has this gesture of mine which put a stop to all that torment been an act of penance then? Had that diabolical whistling been imposed for reasons unknown to me? And now I am sitting quiet at my table, writing, recording it all, and as I do so, in order to re-conjure that exquisitely terrible moment, I remind myself of its intensity by pursing my lips and, very gently, blowing.

CCXCV

I do not try to imagine her here before she arrives, standing before me in this room, as if ready to be appraised by my eyes. I know the day that she is due to come – needless to say, it is always the same day – but I do not look out for her with curiosity or impatience as the hour approaches. I remember all too well the gestures that she makes when she wields mop, duster or broom, and I recall her few words, the few words that we exchange, always, which are, needless to say, polite and perfunctory. I remember the musicality of her voice. Yes, I do remember the strange musicality of her voice, and it is engaging. It brings back to me a snatch of a tune, wrested back, none too easily, from nowhere particularly known to me.

CCXCVI

Night, the thickness, the reassurance of close enveloping night, has at last put a stop to everything. This is the end of things, albeit temporarily, it seems to be saying to me. And no longer to see ahead, I must emphasise, is a miracle to me, because when my eyes are open, I cannot restrain myself from seeing behind all my seeing as far as what all that seeing might be telling me, what the objects might be suggesting to me of that which they seem not to speak, if I may describe it so punctiliously. A ceaseless, tireless probing then, which keeps the nerve ends jangling and on edge from second to second, as if no surface, no matter how rough or how smooth, can ever be quite trusted to be what it seemed to be at the beginning. And so when night falls, shuttering off this seen world, which never ceases to look back at me and interrogate my every moment, my every motive, I sigh as deeply as any well might plummet. I sigh deep down into that space of rest – and perhaps even of death – deep down inside me, where there is such a stillness and such a calm and such a peace that it is surely no fit place for the likes of me. And yet it is to that place that I begin to descend when darkness falls about me, albeit temporarily, because darkness quickly finds the capacity to conjure worlds of its own, which are never slow in coming. Darkness, so lulling and reassuring at first, then wrong-foots me.

CCXCVII

It says to me such things as these, barking them out, orders from the depths. Why now this? Why not that then? Whether or whither? The slowest place or the closest of opportunities? Who was she then? I try to grapple with my answers. I blurt. I bluster. I shift about. I dodge. I feint. And still they come at me. Blows hit me glancingly. I stand on my bed, legs trembling, lurching about, close to falling. I fling my arms about at the enemies who surround me. I feel them everywhere about me. I gulp down their foetid breath. I am trapped, cornered, in this house, in this bed, in this village. I am too well known here. A light of pure malevolence that I cannot see is shining too brightly upon me. They will never not find me. What is it then that I must answer to? How long will these interrogations continue? Am I quite as guilty as they seem to wish me to be? Have I not been mistaken for some other? It is much later that I find myself there, collapsed on my bed, still entire, still complete in body. I drag myself to the window. I observe, almost heart-stoppingly, dawn's gentle rising rose of promise. It is peeking at me, so coyly, so tenderly. My eyes brim with tears to see it. And then these same eyes of mine alight on my books, my pens, my stacked heaps of untidy papers. There is something possible here after all. The world itself, in all its fullness, has not been entirely defeated. There is a space here yet, albeit a narrow one, for generosity, for silence, for slow rumination.

CCXCVIII

Bring me then what I have asked you for. The words have not been spoken out loud. She brings it all the same. She carries the plate of food with loving kindness. She has even opened the window to let in new morning, thrown back the shutters to a revelation of dawn light. The breeze blows across my burning cheeks, soothing the skin. She is touching me now, with a delicate tenderness, on forehead, cheek and neck. She is bending over me and even whispering words into my ear. I want my arms to rise up and embrace her, but I do not have the strength in my limbs. She feeds me the soup, spoonful by spoonful. Her head is turned aside as she does so. I would speak to her, I would say her name out loud, if she would only look at me. But she does not look at me. She continues not to look at me. Meanwhile, I grow stronger inside myself. My limbs lengthen and thicken. I teach myself a new resolve. I see more fiercely through my eyes. Already I am watching the world as it grows and gesticulates beyond the window, and she is standing behind me now, arms hanging, hands empty, as I slowly recede from her.

CCXCIX

When I have said as much as ever needs to be said, I stop. I fling down my pen. I know that I am empty. A desperation sets in. My life is over. Everything has been explained. I have emptied out the sack of myself onto the floor. Every last bit of me has been turned out for my scrutiny. I have closed the door on myself and I have walked away. Only food, at such times as these, will satisfy me. I break off chunks of bread, tearing off fistful after fistful like some eager animal. I cram my mouth greedily. I dip bread into wine, and then I begin masticating, furiously. The mechanism of my mouth is continuing apace. The machinery of my body is functioning. The fuel is being flung into the back of the *poêle* with a greedy, no-holds-barred energy.

CCC

I show pity. I embrace the meek, the weak, the lame, the lowly. I watch them as they inherit the kingdom. I am a bystander at their heavenly revelries. I myself have been excluded. I have led them along the path of righteousness, and I have ushered them through the door. I have watched them, with envy, as they have received their welcome. But I myself have been excluded. Pity me then, outcast that I am. I have striven, and I have fallen. No one has come here to rescue me. They have all passed me by. They have all observed me, and found me wanting. Repugnant. The stench of me perhaps, that human stench. The look of disdain. The leanness of me. The unforgivable glance of sheer desperation. All so repugnant. Raising a hand to them has not done the trick. They do not know me. They have never known me. I am wholly excluded from their company. And this is a good thing – here are my sad words of consolation to myself – because, frankly, I loathe them.

CCCI

The mist is rising from the fields. The veil is thrown back to reveal the world of this new morning, which is both wholly familiar and wholly unfamiliar. And I am walking through this mist, finding my way between the houses, those hulking blanknesses, and the cow byre. I am walking at a steady pace, I know not whither, on this gauzy, fresh-minted morning. My legs are finding their way without dictation. I am letting them loose, giving them some slack, to find their way. There is nothing to speak of inside me today. I am an empty vessel, ringing hollowly when I am struck. I have been reduced to nothing other than this simple act of walking ahead into the tentative future of this new morning which is engulfing me, which amounts to a slow and bewildering opening out to that which must finally forever remain inscrutable and unfathomable. I am as desperate and unknowing as a child again, that child who must forever be teetering on the cliff edge of himself. And yet I am not fearful as that child was once fearful. I am not about to be overwhelmed or overthrown by it all. The world will not fall like a brick on my head. I am merely drifting here, contented, as a boat must drift when it has loosed its moorings. Yes, I am merely drifting, contented. I am being transported, along the horizontal. I am being pulled, with the utmost gentleness. I am being teased. Perhaps I am even being beckoned.

CCCII

Who did you say that you were? You sit here beside me without explaining yourself. I do not know your name or your nature. You have asked permission to write a few words on my behalf, and the words that you and I are reading now, these are the words that you are writing. And you are telling us all that you have refused to explain yourself to me because life itself is fresher, lighter, less encumbered, without the burden of explanation. In short, you want to surprise me – you want to surprise us all – by what you are telling me, sentence by sentence. And, it has to be said, I am quite eager to know why you have interrupted me in this way, and what you mean when you say that Paul may have sent you, that you may have come in his stead today. Can that possibly be so? You are so young and so youthful. Your hand moves at such a speed across the paper. Paul, on the other hand, is old and venerable, with a pace to match his age. You smile at me and then you write down your explanation, word for word. I follow it, eagerly. I am the youthful, ageless spirit of Paul, that is what your words are telling me, which in fact tells me almost nothing at all because you write nothing more than that before you rise up from your chair and leave again without apology or further explanation.

I feel now that I must take it all back, all that I have written, because it amounts to all too meagre a little. I am not within sight of any destination. I am floundering in these waters. The words are streaming from me, but in no particular direction, which means that I am treading water, day by day. Day by day I am treading this water. It stagnates. It coagulates. My life is so cold and so unyielding. Today it is the waters of the *Lavoir* that I am treading. Whenever I write the word water, I see that very particular rectangle of water, enclosed within its walls. And it is not so deep after all. It is not by any means unfathomable. When I removed my socks and my shoes and raised my garment to my knees on that day, I discovered that fact. The water, though so chilling cold, rose no higher than my calves. How long exactly was I standing there, staring down into it as though mesmerised, doing nothing but that? Minutes may have passed, entire hours. Many were there with me in that water, though all unseen. There was no one about me, observing. I had made sure that I would not be seen there. I had stood out in the lane, looking up and down, before I had passed through the doorway. I had looked and looked again, jerking my neck back and forth like some fool of a hen. I had listened. I had waited. I had judged the hour correctly. An hour of solitariness and silence. And then, fearful, I had stepped through, and, breathing deeply, I had prepared myself to enter the water, which was cold enough to chill the entire body. Oh how I had shivered and shivered! I deserved to shiver, I told myself that. I did not hesitate to punish myself. Darkness had descended upon me, of the day and of the spirit, before I left again, at a great hurry needless to say.

CCCIV

It began as a small thing, a mere graze to the skin, sitting a little proud of the left forearm, almost circular, red-raw and almost circular. I ignored it. I covered it. I thought nothing of it. And then, whisperingly, it began to demand attention. It invited me to observe how it grew a little. Never a lot. (It continued to show some discretion.) What is more, I could still hide it away. From myself and from the world. I could still live my life without it. And then it began to speak to me more and more, as if wishing to lecture me on the nature of wounds. Of how they gaped. Their significance. Their purpose. This is no such wound, I began to remonstrate. This is a small thing, a graze of the skin. It goes no deeper. See for yourself how it happened. I struck my forearm against the side of this desk as I rose. I had caused it myself, I said. It was a wound - if so grandiose a word is to be used – of my own devising. Not so, it replied. I stared at it then. I saw for myself how the red-raw lips of the wound were working. The wound was addressing me. This is a marker, a warning, a proof of that which must surely be, it was saying. Do not underestimate the potency of your wound.

CCCV

I am surrounded by no one but myself, and this is a great relief to me. To be answerable to no one. To patrol the boundaries of my own demesne at a pace which must always please me. You ask me then about conversation. You invite me to transform myself, to multiply my selves, by listening to other voices, voices which must surely lead me elsewhere. I need no such assistance. I have created this entire world for myself, and it feels like a world greater than myself. If I conjure voices from the sky, so be it. That is within my remit. I put words into their mouths, and then I listen, feigning surprise.

I hear myself murmuring again. It is a kind of reverie. Am I speaking to Thomas? Put your hand through this body. Now see it emerge on the other side, unhurried, unbloodied. A miracle then, surely a miracle. It is for this reason that they do not see me then. I am transparent. They are seeing through me. For so long I had thought that they, always so fearful and so awe-struck in my presence, were wrapping me about with reverence. Otherwise, why always so tentative? And then one morning I woke up to observe my own arm losing all its density, all its thickness, little by little, as the sun shone down steadily upon it. It was as if the sun was slowly sucking the weight, the mass, the solidity from my flesh until there would be nothing left to be seen at all. I was beginning to stare through myself. I became fearful then, that this disease would spread elsewhere, that the sun would gradually consume the least little part of me until I would be nothing at all. And, last of all perhaps, it would remove from me the capacity to think and to feel so that even as my hand was beginning to falter over this sheet of paper, everything – these words, my seeing – would be drifting away from me. I would know nothing then. And I would be nothing. I would have quite vanished from the world. But no, it seemed to stop just then, part way through its experiment, as if recognising my fears, and wishing to reassure me. The sun hid behind a cloud, and I was restored to myself – but not always, and not forever. When I choose to sit in the sunlight on a day such as this one, I know that once again I am beginning to disappear from the world to such an extent that they no longer have the capacity to see me, these people from the village, these people who have always known me. I know that by the way they seem to look through me as they pass by. It is as if I no longer exist for them in the body. It is as if I have long since been superseded. Terrified then, I hurry back indoors in order to pre-empt my own disappearance. I would bide here a little longer. That would be my greatest wish.

CCCVII

Now I find myself saying it, day after day, as if still crediting my own frail words: I have travelled no great distance to this place. It is always here with me, grounding me, defining me, supporting me. And yet it was not always so. Once there was a newness, a strangeness about it. I could not find my way around it. It surprised me, once, and then again, and then again, with all its crannies, its quaintnesses, its swooping darknesses, its moments of near magical illumination. I would step down into the coldness of the *cave*, groping about, and having felt for and then seized hold of the window embrasure with my hands, I would fling back the single wooden shutter, letting in a sudden shaft of light from the garden. Shocked by the pleasure of it all, the house felt vigorous to me then, alive with my life, and I was consumed, wholly, by a mood of expectancy. It was as if we were adventuring together. My eyes were darting everywhere, and my brain was sparking from the newness of it all. God walked with me in those days, and we talked, constantly. He never failed to answer me when I called upon him. He was forever at my back and my beck. His hand rested upon my hand, quieting me. I had not so much as begun this writing. All this writing came after, years later, by which time I had begun to falter, to topple. I needed to ask myself what was happening then, in those later, darker days. I needed to explain myself to myself. I needed to interrogate the very walls of this house, once so solid, once so dependable.

CCCVIII

Must it continue? It must forever continue. And yet this body will not continue. This body, even as I write down these words at this desk in front of this window – I say it all over again in order to convince myself, and you must forgive me for that – is failing to persevere. It is giving up the ghost on me. It is faltering as if it no longer knows how, who or whither. It is in shock. It is no longer seeing ahead as it once used to see. And I am not talking about the piercingness of the vision, the fact, for example, that certain gargoyles, raised up so high, are no longer visible to me from this window. I am talking about spiritual penetration, that slow and profound seeing into the depths of things. Once upon a time I was more capable than I am today – or at the very least I believed myself to be more capable. My book-learning spirited me on. I was capable, with such seeming ease, of encompassing worlds of my own imagining. In short, I was more fully, more completely, in control of myself. That is no longer the case. I rise up to nothing but a flurry of questions now, nothing but questions. I no longer have any answers. The answers, once so abundant, have all slipped away. My answers have all transformed themselves into questions, and without my even noticing. I have been foolishly serene, somnolently serene, in my self-assurance, my confidence, even as the answers have been slipping away from me. And now I stand on my step, looking out, blankly, and the wind blows chill, and I do nothing but wrap my arms about me.

CCCIX

Sometimes when I speak to you, you are present, vividly present, to me, and we engage in pressingly eager conversation, than which nothing matters more to me. We are so abundantly present to each other. I walk around you. I point in your direction, as if to single you out. I smile into your face, and you smile back at me, as if encouraging me to continue. And I do continue because on this day, at this particular hour, I am so eager to please you. I am so eager to coax those persuasive looks of warmth and encouragement from you. It is at such hallowed times as these that I know you will never leave me, that you will be forever as present to me as you are on this day, my day of days, with its rising note of festivity and its random pleasures. And then, almost without warning – perhaps there is some cloud cover, perhaps that should be regarded as premonitory – you seem to be slipping away from me. I am standing here, talking as usual, but your words are no longer filling in the spaces between my words. With the consequence that I begin to speak less eagerly, and less persuasively to you. You are no longer that model of attentiveness, hope and reassurance. And then I plant my two legs in front of you, determined to engage you. I shout into your face. Your body does not respond to me. It has slackened. Your mouth refuses to open. And even as I stare at you, your features are slipping away from me, absenting themselves from your body, as if they were nothing but a breath of rising smoke on the air. In fact, all that now remains of you, hanging in the air between myself and the mesmerising stare of the window, is that familiar stench of cigarette smoke which, even as I look ahead of me, is rising in slow curlicues towards the window, writhing away from me, making its escape. Even if I wished, I could not snatch at you with my hand. I could not bring you back here to continue this conversation. And it is you who have chosen.

CCCX

It is a day like no other, a day of unparalleled ferocity. He is judging. He is condemning. He is scoring out my words. And I accept it all with such meekness. I stand beside him, watching, mute, hands folded in front of me. And then, in the blink of an eye it all changes. I come alive in a different way. I feel myself rising up against him. And now I am writing words in defiance of his wishes. I even fuel his anger by preparing a text which will be anathema to him, a text based on words of his own, a text which dandles with his words as a ball is dandled between the hands by a child. Yes, I have taken his words and I have rearranged them, and I have described this new work as a homage to his genius. His anger rises against me. He does not recognise what I am doing. He does not recognise this to be an act of quite deliberate and calculated

provocation. Perhaps even a tease of sorts. He scores my words through with his pen, savagely. He destroys the little that I have made of him. There is therefore a distance between us now, a wedge of quite considerable proportions. And it pleases me that this should be so. His savagery has quickened my courage. I see that it is all possible now, that I can define myself against him, that I can stand back from him and judge his words and his deeds as wanting. I am capable of playing his game. I am even able to stand in his stead or to rise higher by sitting on his shoulders. I can see myself through his eyes – should I so wish. I can condemn myself and find myself wanting. And then begin again elsewhere, as someone else, wholly unknown to him, and wholly uncaring. He has flung open so many entry points to my life. I am spoilt for choice.

CCCXI

I have begun again. The words are moving more quickly now, streaming from this pen like the gush of a mountain stream, almost unstoppable. And the faster they spue out of me, the more they seem to be urging me forward in my thinking. There will be new explanations, new clarities, new definitions, I am promised. I am young today, leaping, cart-wheeling young, and even child-like in my impulsive swiftness. I have such spirit that I have even chosen to ignore the appearance of this ageing, forward stooping body. All this oldness, all this decrepitude, they are an illusion, the mirror's illusion, a voice is telling me, so raucous and so insistent. I am re-making my own life, minute by minute. And here is the proof it. She is standing in front of me, welcoming me, and even preparing my bed for me. The journey from there to here has been a long one, and now here she is at last, come, as any mother would come, to soothe away all my cares. And the first thing that she does is to prepare my bed for me. She lies across it, warming it through, in preparation for my body. And when I go to lie down after her, my body fits perfectly into the warm shape of her own body. Even that smile of hers is still with me, lingering about me in this room long after she has left me, appearing to pattern the very walls, a regular repeated pattern of opening lips which I am able to touch, one by one, when I reach out my hand with weary pleasure... And none of this is illusory, none of this is the first in an infinite series of vain wishes which will go stretching ahead of me, as a child will often choose to run in front of another, forever outpacing him.

CCCXII

Could this really be true, that I came alive to myself only after witnessing the beginning of my own life? It was as if I was seeing myself being born, standing to one side of that bed, watching how they handled me when I slipped forth, and how they then slapped me across the buttocks and raised me up. And that has continued. I have lived my life retrospectively. It has always streamed on ahead of me, unknown to me, and I have come limping after, calling out its name, to which it has so seldom responded... Only much later have I preyed upon my every decision, scrutinising its rightness, its truthfulness, asking myself whether or not it was consistent with everything else that I have known of my own life as I have lived it day by day. To know is no easy matter. We arrive in ignorance of ourselves and of all that which surrounds us. Life is a fearful blankness, the prospect of a terrible hazarding. There is a slow and steady groping forward. Illumination of any kind is always a long way ahead of us. We know the word, we hallow it as we hallow so many things that are unknown to us, but we are seldom within reach of its meaning. I have a head cold today, and this affliction has been driving the thoughts of this day, so confused and so troubling. I am experiencing a terrible thickening inside my own head. It feels as blockish and as unyielding as hard wood. When I yawn, my jaws squeak like an old door pushed back for the first time in years. My seeing is a mist of seeing. My eyelids weigh upon my eyeballs. Even the morning coffee, my daily solace, has not consoled me.

CCCXIII

Let me confess this to you then, as honestly as I am able. I am nothing more than a man amongst men, puny, risible, lacking in all distinction. I cannot inflate myself. I cannot rise higher than my own height. Nor can I shrink to the size of a shoe box. I am only what I am and what I have always been, and this fact has always disappointed me because the promise was that in the fullness of time I would become greater than this smallness, that I would exceed myself. God's benediction would ensure such an advancement. I was after all his messenger and he, being my guardian, my stay and my guide, would see to it. He would raise me up until I became an enviable custodian of the needy, a man to be singled out amongst men. It has not happened. I have remained doggedly the same, life-long. That raising up was an illusory promise. In fact, if anything I have shrunk inside myself. I am smaller now, more knotted, more compacted in my ugliness, of both body and spirit. I am a thing wholly self-regarding. In short, I am a great disappointment to myself.

CCCXIV

The gate has been torn from its hinges by the violence of the storm which raged throughout the night. I listened to it intently from beneath the blankets, hour after long hour. I took some courage from all that display of violence. It lent a certain keenness of appetite to my night-hours' musings. I felt a little bolder and stronger inside myself. It was as if the force of the wind was driving me on, lifting me up, and even bearing me to the very pinnacle of the temple, from where I could survey, calm and imperious, the slow, lazy progress of the world beneath my gaze. It was not until I rose from my bed in the morning that I saw how it had torn off the garden gate from its hinges and then, naturally enough, I cursed it. There are few things worse than wanton destruction.

CCCXV

Stay with me now, for a little while longer. I hear myself speaking these words, over and over, whisperingly. I feel my lips mouthing. I even touch my parched lips in order to prove to myself that it must surely be true, what it is that I am saying, these incantatory words, over and over, at such an hour as this one, this hour between hours, when I feel myself to be neither fully living nor fully dying: stay with me now. Yes, it is these words that I am intoning. And I see you standing there at the bed's head, faintly, or is it perhaps beside me, within reach of me when I stretch out my hand to you... Just so. And your mouth is opening to respond to me, I see how it is opening, and your eyes are widening to receive me. That is what the look in your eyes seems to be saying, that, yes, you will receive me, yes, you will hear me, yes, you will respond to me. That there is no longer this great and unbridgeable distance between us, that you have arrived at my bedside without warning, when I was not so soundly sleeping. As ever, I was not so soundly sleeping, and you have known all along the reason for my restlessness, you have known along that it is because I have always wanted you, and now you have come to fill this void, this absence, with the fullness of yourself, without warning. And I am so restless to have you here with me.

CCCXVI

How to explain the strange emptiness of this new day, the feeling that this day has already passed away, its spirit quite vanished, even before it has arrived here to be with me? And yet it is I who must surely create this new day. I am entirely responsible for this new

day being what it is, whether that be bright or sullen, light or ponderously heavy about my shoulders. Who is there other than myself to blame for the new day being what it is? Can this really be true though? This new day feels wholly set apart from me when I descend these stairs, with such heavy, dragging, wearisome steps, to the kitchen in order to prepare my consolatory bowl of coffee. It is not a day of my making. It exists here quite apart from me. It stands here ready to receive me, and if it looks at me blankly, stonily, who is there to blame for any of this? Am I then being chastised by this new day for being who I am, for finding myself here yet again, between my arrival and my departure, not knowing what lies ahead of me? Am I to be blamed for the mood of this new day? Or have those clouds, in all their sullenness, their low broodingness, made me everything that I am today? Have they caused me to turn upon myself in this way, to reject all that I have ever been, to refuse to see that there is any path ahead of me? The truth must surely lie somewhere, I am muttering to myself as I raise my legs exaggeratedly high in order to restore a little circulation to my cold and blockish toes. Oh, would that I might feel my toes again! If I could feel the ends of my toes, perhaps all would be well. Perhaps all manner of things would be well. Now I am almost smiling, and the sun is almost inveigling its presence into this kitchen, giving a dull sheen to the *carrelage* beneath my feet.

CCCXVII

I would and yet I cannot. I would and yet I cannot. Every fibre of my being seems to offer up some resistance. I would speak through the words of this prayer, which are so familiar to me. I would draw on this prayer if I could as one draws on a snugly comfortable glove, feeling myself warmed and protected by the familiarity of its words. I would enter the family of this prayer, finding it ready to receive me with such enveloping gestures of welcome. And yet I cannot. This does not happen. I am reading nothing but words,

words, words in front of my eyes, one after another, words in slow, drilling, orotund succession, words which lack intimacy, words which stand proudly apart from me, words which fail to envelop me. I have not written these words. These words do not belong to me. These words are not a part of my life. When these words knock on the door of my heart, with such a furious insistence, I refuse to admit them. I must reach out for other words, words of my own choosing. Or perhaps I can mismanage the same words, with relish.

CCCXVIII

I have caught it in my web. And now I am examining it, from all sides, by the light of this new morning. The sentences were spinning on apace, quite giddily, and then, at a certain moment, they came to a sudden and abrupt halt. A single word was standing in the way of my bowling, careering sentences, telling me to stop and consider. And that word was flighty, which is undoubtedly a curiosity, as I recognised immediately, because the word itself seems to encourage me to run on as speedily as my life is prepared to carry me. It suggests lightsomeness, gaiety, headlong propulsion in combination with jocularity, airborne cavortings and sleights of hand... And now here it sits, mighty as a boulder, blocking the onward flow of this tiny rill of my words...

CCCXIX

You have never asked me to give an account of myself, I declare that now. All this is entirely voluntary. These wings are fashioned from wax, and they will surely perish in the heat of the sun. I work against the grain of my own life. I am squeezing myself as hard as a lemon is squeezed. Every last drop of the juice of me must be forced to give a full and truthful account of itself.

CCCXX

Lock the door at night, as on every other night in this house, in this world of every new day's dying at its close. Turn the ponderous key in the lock, with a single anti-clockwise leftward turn, and then slip the key into the trouser pocket, feeling it slide past the coolness of the flesh of the upper thigh. Twist the body away from the door. Two or three paces then, just as far as the box on the mantel. Tweak the key from the pocket between thumb and first finger, easy does it now because it has been known to fall back, and then dandle it in the palm somewhat for the sheer pleasure of doing so, judging the weight, feeling the heft of it, before deftly lifting the lid of the box (with the other hand), and then placing the key, with great care, horizontally, in the bottom of the box, laying it to rest, with great care, as one might settle a body recently passed from the perils of this life, once and forever, in the darkness of the sepulchre, not to be raised again until the trumpet, unanswerable, unavoidable, sounds for one and all on that day of days we know not when. Not so with this hefty metal key though. This key will be raised up again when the new light, the light of new morning, comes calling, playfully. Then the lid will yawn back squeakily, and the key will once again be raised into the light of new-minted morning, in the left hand as on so many occasions before, and it will be slipped back into the left-hand trouser pocket in order to begin its steady, two or three steps' journey – no more than that – which is over and done in the blink of an eye – to the door of the house, where it will be inserted, vertically, into the lock, and there it will be slowly turned, to the right, and the bolt, that snug-fitting, iron bolt, with an uncomfortable grind in its throat, will slide back, on cue, and the key, then, will have done its job. And the door will be open.

CCCXXI

My friends, my Sunday friends, I know you for what you are in so far as you vouchsafe to me the truth about yourselves. It is as much as I shall ever know of the truth of your lives. When you are laid to rest, in the aftermath of your solemn burials, I pace for a moment or two about the straitness, the meanness of your houses, in the company of your grieving friends and neighbours, your few broken dear ones, a small strew of them, awash with grief in my steadying company. They too scarcely knew you, let me hazard. You exchanged words with them throughout your life, but they were common words, words plucked from the earth, words plucked from the hedgerows. So much wild fruit. They were never words particular to you. You had no such words. No such words had ever grown inside you. There was a great windy void inside you, which was why I never knew you, because there was nothing to be known about you – except perhaps that sweetest of sweet smiles when you carried a posy in your fist and offered it to me, a small posy of wild flowers, hedgerow flowers, accompanied by two stray words, no more than that, words that I had said to you, years before, words which you were now returning to me, with gracious thanks, words, it has to be said, that I had quite forgotten. I accepted it from you, that posy, when you thrust it towards me, quite awkwardly, as if you would be rid of it. I even returned smile for smile. By the hour of our next engagement, you had been laid to rest, and I was solemnising over you, as any priest must surely do.

CCCXXII

I do not proclaim it to one and all. I do not say it out loud. I do not tell them that I am broken into small and tragic pieces, which now lie here, willy nilly, strewn about this floor like the parts of some shattered Dresden figurine. Occasionally I kick at one or another of these fragments, large or small, quite venomously. I do not know

whether, were I to gather them all together, they could be re-assembled. I have not tried to count them. When I walk about this village, when I lean out from the pulpit, fulminating, when I listen to my own voice and hear how it rises up in the direction of heavenly heights or how it descends towards the hellish depths at the stir of inward anger, I make no reference to the fact that this body, so seemingly entire and of a whole, this black clothed body which paces in front of them or blesses them with a raised hand, is no longer who or what it seems to be. Who or what? That is perhaps a matter for another day. I do not invite them to carry off small parts of me – an ear lobe perhaps, an eyeball, a finger end, or perhaps even a single eye lash – in order to make this grotesque object the hallowed centrepiece of some family shrine, settled in the unwholesome company of the other random meannesses of their miserable lives. I do not invite them to divide me into a multiplicity of glorious relics. That would be too much. That would be quite ridiculous. And yet perhaps it would be all to the good. At least I would have done with myself once and for all, at least I would be no longer hanging here over this sheet of paper, at this desk beside this window, brooding obsessively, and quite nonsensically, upon the frivolous excesses of humankind.

CCCXXIII

I have no wish to call you back here. Your afternoon's work is over and done. The *carrelage*, slippery, wet-gleams beneath my feet. You have made all things new. You have made all things tidy and just so. You are a mistress of the neat double-fold. And I am grateful to you, always, for all your ministrations. You are doing me a great service. I do not expect more than this from you. I do not expect you to close the kitchen door slowly after you, as though you might be expecting to stay a little longer, as though you were leaving with a modicum of reluctance. I do not expect to hear your feet dragging just a little as you descend the steps to the gravel.

And, most of all, I do not expect you to look back in this direction as you pull the garden gate closed behind you, with a firm snap. I do not expect you to raise your head to this window where I am standing, looking out, after you have closed the gate behind you. I do not expect you to glance in this direction, and to see me staring back at you, wonderingly. I do not expect you to give me the faintest of faint smiles as you stand there, for no longer than the briefest of brief moments, with your hand resting lightly on the top of the gate. And you do not do so. And, more to the point, I am not looking out for you.

CCCXXIV

He lies so still on the surface of the water, which is untroublingly calm this morning, afloat on his back, outstaring the sun. When he has a mind, he flips his young and agile body over, agile and sleek as a seal, and begins to swim out in the direction of the horizon, arms churning the waves into a fury. I fear for him. He does not fear for himself because he is a child of the water. He is in his element. The water is his settled environment. And he will in time be buried beside this water because there was nothing but love between them. I, on the other hand, when I lower my fingers to the water of this sink, shiver in anticipation. Even to write the word – water – makes me fearful.

CCCXXV

I find myself waking up in anticipation, night after night, at all hours of the night. I am being harried. I sit upright, clutching at the edges of the bed in order to steady myself. I speak out. I listen to my own voice as it pushes back against the darkness. I hear my own outbreathed words hanging hesitant in the air. There is a little gentle soughing of the wind perhaps. Nothing more than that. There is the moon's bright, white interrogatory eye perhaps.

Nothing more than that. Otherwise nothing and no one. And yet I am being carried ahead on invisible wings, towards the door, and I cannot prevent its happening. I cannot push away from myself this belief that when he arrives, I will admit him, and that he will then proceed to contradict every certitude that I have ever possessed. The nature of my life – such as it is. The scope of my doubts. It will all be overturned, and I will be left with nothing.

CCCXXVI

There is a book that I have lost. There is a book that I have forgotten. Stray words reach out to me, words from that book, inscrutable words of great significance. I examine every book that I possess. It is not amongst them. I try to remember its author, its title. The details elude me. They always elude me. I remember the fact of it, its massiveness, the gilded edges of its pages. I remember how it spoke to me, night after night, at the hour of sleep, and of how I gorged on it until I was full to overflowing. Nothing filled me quite so full as that book, nothing in heaven or on earth. And now it has left me. Now it wholly eludes me. Now it has chosen to play cat and mouse games with me. The odd word. The odd phrase. They fall down through the air to tease me, to tempt me, to taunt me, when I am least expectant. At such times – and it is on days when I have usually reconciled myself to its loss – they return to me, piercing me like barbs, accusing me not so much of wilful forgetfulness as of neglect, unpardonable neglect.

CCCXXVII

Let me acknowledge the truth of it to myself. Day by day I am thinning and thinning. It is age, advancing age, which has done this to me, and there is no answer. There is only submission. There is nothing but the closure of the eyes and the steady onward breathing. My rotundity once gave me such pleasure. I rolled as I walked. I swayed from side to side. I proceeded, stately, ever oncoming, ever to be prepared for. They stepped aside. They acknowledged, without ever quite declaring, the significance of the bulk of my arrival. I brought pressure to bear upon every proceeding by the sheer forward thrust of the stomach. Now all that has slipped away from me. It is as if slice after slice has been sheered off me, mercilessly, unfeelingly, by some butcher's keen-edged blade, leaving me hanging here so lean and so spectral that I am now imagining myself to be the ghost of myself, preying upon the past of everything that I once amounted to. Needless to say, this spectral thinness adds to my fearfulness. It says to me: there is so little now, so small a space, between this world and the next. I test my voice against the air in order to prove to myself that there still exists a modicum of substance, that I possess the power, still, to bring a little pressure to bear upon the world. Alas, even my shout has diminished. No dog flinches from me. I cock an ear to a tepid bark from behind a gate. Another slinks away, disinterested.

CCCXXVIII

And so it has happened. And so it will happen. I must not fall victim to false anticipation. That would be reckless, an all-too-casual throw of the dice. I must not ransack the fusty, dusty attic room of old memories, picking about at random, endeavouring to make sense of it all. And so here I stand, miserable monument that I am, sufficient unto the day. Being only who or what I am. Weighed here in the balance by my own conscience and little else. All the whisperings from the corners have fallen away. There are no stray nods of encouragement to be attending to. I am no longer the victim of random sleights of hand. Nor do I stand ready here to be pitied by you and you. I have done what I have done. I have seen all that I have seen. I have pinned a name to myself, and I have learnt to utter that name with a measure of spurious authority.

CCCXXIX

Yes, the day of reckoning is every new day that remains to me. It is the ceaselessly frenetic examination of all that has been said or written or spoken. There is to be no postponement, no hesitation, no return to the beginning. And yet on every new day - as now, once again – the beginning strives to break through. The child that I once was, that helpless, carefree thing, endeavours to assume control of me, and to make its voice heard once again. It is striving all over again to make a plea for innocence, to tell me that nothing matters now, and that nothing need weigh upon me because there is really nothing to be known except the bowling of a hoop along a lane or the tossing of a coloured ball from hand to hand. This is perfection – the words din inside my ears – it is telling me, do not ignore such blissful ignorance as this. And I willingly take the hand of this child who is speaking to me, who is closer to me now than my own hectic breathing, and I walk ahead with him a little way until the shadows begin to fall, and then I hesitate, and, lo, all the future begins, which is even now continuing. I am so completely lost to the innocence of myself, and I would surely be magicked there if only I could.

CCCXXX

This world that I am seeing from the window is not exactly the same world as yesterday. It is the lightest of light skims across the surface of what may or may not constitute the reality of my own life, the life that I have created for myself in this place. And yet I stillhesitate to tear it away. What is more, I believe that I do not even have the strength to tear it away, let us not pretend. And so I am learning to live with it again. I am learning to accept it for the all that it will ever be to me, and that is a comfort because within that line of sight there is also my own hand. I can see my own hand resting on the edge of this window, and that hand is a part of everything, it is at one with – it is a continuation of – those rooftops and the gently falling ground beyond when I choose to look to see. And so I fully understand that were I to rip that veil away – as it is not within my capacity to do – I would also rip away my own hand. I would remove the very hand that is now telling you these things, that is describing to you, with the aid of this pen, this world of mine, in all its evanescence and all its circumscription. And so I would be left with nothing. I would not even be capable of describing myself as a floating shadow or, perhaps somewhat worse, as the merest blink-and-then-gone.

CCCXXXI

Help me then. Wrest me from this all-encompassing darkness, as you would rescue a child, some mewling, squirming bundle flung over a shoulder, from a burning building. Come to my aid. Bring me my sword, my staff of faith, my scrip. None of these things are with me now. My scrip is empty, quite void of all its good and tasty morsels. My sword is rusting away in the corner. And yet the ability to conjure these things with words quickens me all over again. It leads me in the direction of a mood of excitable anticipation. I am coming alive again. I am beginning to experience – oh the pomp, the rodomontade of mere words! – the plenitude of my own life. It enables me to see that sword in my hand once again, swinging, swingeing... It enables me to eat from my scrip, to gorge on all those tasty morsels, until I am strong and ready to resume the journey that must surely lie ahead of me, life-long.

CCCXXXII

Good neighbourliness is as nothing to me. I have nothing in common with the man who arrives at the gate, exhausted, hand extended. I offer him a little help. I go through the motions. I touch a grimy, sweat-soaked forehead. I say a brief prayer. I give a perfunctory blessing, the least flurry of the hand, the fingers. It is more than sufficient. And then he shuffles away from me, adequately recompensed. I have sustained him in the spirit. I have given him a smidgen of hope, which is a not entirely unwelcome companion on a journey such as his. And yet he is nothing to me. Chaff blown on the wind. I never look into another man's eyes. Were I to do so, I would see only myself reflected back at me, staring at myself, pitying myself for the limitations that I am obliged to suffer until the end of this wearisome journey.

CCCXXXIII

Our help in ages past. His very absence now excites me. It puts me on my mettle. I know that life is this terrible hazarding, this groping ahead into ever thicker mists of uncertainty. I am my own keeper, my own guardian, the custodian of my own conscience.

CCCXXXIV

The weather, in all its headlong fury, has entirely encompassed this house. For so many long hours now this fragile house has been a prey to the circling, ever furiously circling wind, and now there are hailstones pummelling against the door. Am I in a mood of panic? Would I wish to escape? On the contrary, I am sitting here at this desk watching the rain drive against the window, seeing it streaming down in rivulets as if to entertain me. And I am indeed entertained by all this elemental majesty. It is as if a great symphony has struck up, for my pleasure alone, a symphony infinitely various, and here I sit, comfortably, recording its passing, as if it were the passing of some mighty street procession. And I am a mere child again, fiercely clutching her hand as the lurching crucifix, surrounded by so many, sweeps on by with tremendous solemnity. I see it with such aching clarity, raised up high on its rackety plinth, with the saviour's body, blood streaming from his wounds, slumped over,

and his face, that pallid face, turned towards me, looking at me alone, seeing deep into me, asking questions of me to which, even now, so many years on, I am still struggling to give truthful answers.

CCCXXXV

I have passed beyond the need for food. I am even refusing to acknowledge the meaning of the word. When I have it, I stare down at it suspiciously, as if the soup in this bowl has conjured itself into existence in order to do me harm. I stare hard down into its thick, brown, unmoving surface. I see the spoon and how it pierces that surface as a knife might pierce a body, and I am repulsed by such a sight. It would be so much easier, so much more spirit-cleansing, to take no food on this day. My body has risen up against it. We are at warfare because I am in need of no such sustenance. I carry it in its deep ceramic bowl to the sink, and then I tip it at a steep angle to the vertical, seeing its curving pour. I watch it slowly disappear, circling about the hole in the sink, and then streaming down that hole and deep into the earth beneath. I need no such sustenance. As I say these words out loud to myself, as I hear them ringing out on the air like a great proclamation, I feel my body lightening, easing off its burdens. I watch my fingers rising in the air, rising, rising to unassailable heights. I marvel at the sight of my own fingers up there in the heights, frozen in immobility. And then I raise myself up on the tips of my toes. I begin the sacred dance of the un-needy.

CCCXXXVI

I am moaning inside myself. I cannot stop myself. I cannot stop my own body rocking back and forth. I am a child being rocked in its chair. I am utterly helpless now. Time is awash about me, time, with its whirligig of objects, its places (how infinitely various they seem!), and its flighty, passing moments. The whole of my life has flooded in on me this morning, without warning. I am in a mood of near unutterable desperation. My hands are as if attached to the arms of this chair. I cannot separate out, one from another, all these particles of air. I cannot make sense of it all, there is too much mayhem, too much clamour, too many random, wasted words from too many voices. There are far too many circumambient voices. The living and the dead are equally alive within me, appealing, open-mouthed, for my attention, accusing me, every last one, of having neglected them. My grandmother stands at the bed head, flourishing her apron, and my father stands beside her, sentinel-like, frowning down at me. I go to speak to them. The words, few and ragged at the edges, all fail me. I have always dealt in words of so little consequence. This window to which I have now been introduced, when I press back against it, feels infinitely malleable. I lick off the few passing streaks of rain because I am fearfully thirsty. I am above all thirsting for peace, silence, a little quietude. I am thirsting to be gone from here. Is it not possible to set fire to a chair such as this one at my back, that dear old familiar? Is it not possible for a human being such as I am to disappear in a puff of smoke, and then to heave a sigh of gratitude at my own absence? And now Marie is here again – I watch her feet shifting here and there about the floor. She is shaking a duster in front of my face as I sit here in this chair. It is a little too close for comfort.

CCCXXXVII

It is the passing rain, so casually passing, which is blowing into my face appealingly. It has caught at the edge of my cheek as I walk towards the door of the church. Its coolness, its lightness – these are welcoming signs. I have the cold, heavy key in my pocket. I dandle it in my hand, unseen. The light rain, the cooling, appeasing rain is still driving against me. It has not forgotten me. It is still so pleasingly attentive. I feel how it pricks at my eyelids. It is giving me the lightest of light kisses.

CCCXXXVIII

And now, having fleeted over the graveyard relatively light of foot (stepping within yards of the War Memorial), I have arrived at the portal of this church once again in order to announce myself. I am standing in the doorway, as if shouldering its great stone arch. I wait for my moment. I watch for a furtive eye to glance in my direction. They are all kneeling as they should, faces pressed into palms, tacitly musing upon the solemnity of it all, duly cowed by my presence here. And it is of course nothing new, my presence here. I come and I go like the passing seasons. I wax and I wane like the moon. They know me so well that they barely heed me at all. I am an old glove, worn for a little while, on days of inclement weather perhaps, and then tossed aside. And yet still, and in spite of the numbing inevitability of it all, I choose to enter this place of high solemnity, believing myself to be this walking man of great reserve and high solemnity, who is here now, at this hour, on this day of days – a day much like any other, it has to be said before you say it for me – because it is needful that things happen in this way. If things were not to happen in this way, a great blankness would supervene. I would find myself kneeling, and lamenting, in some far corner, and no one would see me there, least of all myself. No one would be reaching out to me with a measure of consolation.

CCCXXXIX

It is as if a great hammer is pummelling me. I wake up with a jolt. Something of consequence must surely be happening. And yet I am nowhere other than here, pinioned here in my own bed, motionless. And yet I am also utterly breathless, and trembling, as if I had been running – and am perhaps still running – a great race whose finishing line will never arrive. My heart is speeding, thundering within this chest cavity, making my ribs bounce like a ball, filling me with fear that my heart might burst at any moment.

And there is no palpable reason for any of this. Was I not lost in deepest sleep, untroubled by dreams? No voices were calling out to me. I was not disturbed by any knock on the door. And this is not the first time such an assault has happened. In fact, it is at such moments as this, when I seem to be sleeping dreamlessly, that the forces of unreason seize hold of me, as if knowing me to be at my most helpless, alone as I am in this bed with none here to protect me, to save me from fear's random arrows. How they have come now, a great storm of them, teeming down through the air to pierce me. Would that I could fathom the source of all this random torment. Would that I could understand why I deserve such punishment, I, I, I who am little more than a mere nothing.

CCCXL

I lost those beauteous hours somewhere, those hours that were once so very particular to me, hours in the course of which I had arrived at some satisfactory explanation, to the extent that I smiled to myself because I knew then that the lock had clicked shut at last, and I had reached my destination, that place I had always desired to be. And I still see myself, albeit faintly now, at that moment of full realisation, that instant of plenitude, when everything was at last revealed to me, and I could at last relax back into myself, allowing all the random pains and the small ghostly tauntings of the body to fade away, as the pains of the body do melt away from time to time, when we sit lolling in a chair in the garden perhaps, at some fleeting instant of full summer's sunlight, when the sun plays gently about the skin. It is at such moments as these that the entire world seems to be at one. And now, on this day, I find myself reaching back to that elusive moment, oh so eager to find it again, when all was finally resolved and set forth. And it happened – this must surely be true, as surely true as the sight of my hand moving across this sheet of paper on this new day's morning of dappled autumnal sunlight – during those hours that I have now mislaid, albeit perhaps temporarily.

CCCXLI

I have not yet lost my superior understanding of this makeshift
world. I am still capable of deploying these words, of drawing
multiple arrows from this quiver. They still cause the earth to
tremble at my feet. They still ring forth. They still urge the clouds
to go scudding about the sky. Silly, self-duped old man. Blinder by
the passing hour. Stiff and yet stiffer of limb. Less resolute. Less
forthright. In the clutch of such timidity that when I go to open the
door, I sniff nothing but fear and danger in the air. And yet there is
no apparent danger out there. All is as somnolent as ever. The
world and all its dangers are almost entirely absent. Why is it then
that I conjure a predator from every slight and passing breeze?
Draw in the limbs for a little while yet, my friend. Erase the face.
Close fast the box.

CCCXLII

Why does reason make such unreasonable demands upon me?
Am I not equal to the passing hour? I was at first a nothing, a mere
wisp, an afterthought, a forgotten promise, an unwelcome surprise.
No one asked for me to happen. On a certain day I chose to
interpose myself between you and you. Do you remember how the
earth trembled? I jest, of course. No one anticipated the smallness
of my contribution to this world. I was obliged to create a little
space for myself, and I did so, with great unwillingness, which
provoked a measure of resentment, to which I responded with
bruisings and rancour and, finally, indifference. I am indifferent in
exactly the way that the clouds are indifferent.

CCCXLIII

You stood before me this morning, blocking out the light. Your voice was a singing voice, shrill, high above me. I reached up to you. It was insufficient. And now I am recording, as carefully as I am able, the lineaments of your face. I am being as slavishly accurate as I am capable of being. And you are, little by little, appearing to me once again, as if willing yourself to be here with me. Only your words are missing. I am obliged to guess at your words.

CCCXLIV

Night speaks of the peacefulness of night. It whispers its words of comfort into my ear, its few words, so slow and so halting. I am suitably nurtured and sustained. I would lie here forever, gently embalming myself. Then a restlessness seizes hold of me. I turn over and then over once again, like an ever shifting dog. There is surely a certain position in this bed which will feel most appropriate, and which is waiting for me to find it. Once found, it will be known, and I will then be at peace, with the night wrapped about me, with this singular night wrapped like a blanket about me, like this blanket which presently covers me so thinly. Nothing else must reach me. I would listen to no one's words but my own. All else is a matter of indifference to me. I say that to myself over and over.

CCCXLV

Say it now, and say the words quickly. Let them come hurrying towards me, like children with their begging bowls. And I will be ready for them. I will be standing here, at the gate, open-handed, to welcome them, to welcome this new flock of words. They will become a part of me, very quickly. I will accustom them to my habits. I will teach them about myself. I will introduce myself to

them. And, little by little, they will come to understand me. They will adapt themselves to this close and intimate environment, because that is what it is here, so close and so intimate. There is nothing of the wider world hereabouts. All that must fall away. They must adapt themselves to the stricter measure of this world. It will be good for them. They will learn to live again.

CCCXLVI

Priestliness is my carapace. No looking behind, mind you. No beastly probings or proddings. No piercings of the veil. That is forbidden, and even to myself. I must be what I must be, and this is all that you would expect of me. I must never fall away from myself. I must never topple and shatter into a thousand miserable and incomprehensible fragments. I must remain, forever, this upright monument, solid, rigid, irrefrangible, a witness, a testimony, to all that I am believed to be. And to all that I believe myself to be? Perhaps. Perhaps not. Encircle me for a little while. Encircle me until you go dizzy. As long as I stand here, totemic, unquenchable, I will not disappoint you.

CCCXLVII

Tomorrow is such an unlikely opportunity. I have never dealt in tomorrows. They do not exist for me. They are not solid ground. I cannot comprehend the scope of their possibilities because I have never found myself there to enjoy them. I am only and forever here, trapped here in this moment like a rat in a cage, staring out through the bars with my coal-black eyes. Tomorrow, by comparison, must forever be so sweet and so winsome. It is the kingdom of fumy forgetfulness, where life consists of a thousand driftings hither and thither, and I would never quite hear what was being said because tomorrow, being itself, would surely be forever turned away from me. What is more, I have no wish to burst in and claim it for myself. I would not know it. I would not know myself. I would look back, fearful, and see myself here, so far away and so helpless, pleading for my return to this safe haven, my only and forever place.

CCCXLVIII

Were I ever to fall, would you be ready to run and to catch me? Were I to fall and to break into that thousand fragments, would you feel a certain responsibility towards me? Or would you pass me by on the other side of the lane, hurrying away? Which means, of course, that no one in this world is dependable because I do not possess the air of a needy man. I lack the general demeanour of a man of flesh and blood. I am a man of the spirit. I spirit through their lives, without a single glance to left or to right. I pronounce upon higher things – matters of life and death, for example. I do not meddle with their daily tomfooleries. I am most certainly not a certain man amongst men.

CCCXLIX

I have no idea just how long I was waiting for you here. I have not counted the minutes, the hours, the days. All is so immeasurable. All is in such a state of flux. Nothing pins me to this world through which I seem to drift and scheme. All I know – and I know this for sure, as I would know a rock at my feet – is that I was waiting for you with an infinity of patience, and that I was so concentrated upon that act of patient waiting that I lost sight, wholly, of who or what you were. Had anyone asked me just then, had anyone chosen to interrupt all that patient waiting, I would not have been able to conjure you or describe you. I would not have been able to explain why I was waiting with such patience beside this door or this window. All I would have said, had I been asked, is something like this: there is a great gulf here – I would have pointed to that gulf, indicating how it stretched out before me – and I am waiting for it to be filled. Hence such patience. Hence such an infinity of patience. In fact, that never happened. No one enquired. No one showed the smallest degree of curiosity. And I am still waiting. I am still waiting for you here.

CCCL

Who are you then? Let me ask myself that question. Let me also ask you that question. Who will be the first to answer? The question itself gives me succour. It gives me a reason for being, a reason to leap ahead and claim you as if you were some land to be colonised. Who are you then? Were I to describe you here, it would amount to the crudest of crude approximations because mere words – my words – could never do you justice. Were I to write a poem in praise of you, it would be stuffed full of generalities and borrowed tropes, buoyed along on so much wind. And so I must wait for you to tell me who you are. I must wait for you to make good on that promise to fill to the brim that gulf which yawns inside me. I know that you have made such a promise. I am secure in that knowledge.

CCCLI

If words were not in such contention with words, there might be peace in this place. I hear them jostling and murmuring in the night. I hear how the papers on this desk rise up, rustling, and then slap themselves down again, as if in some act of defiance. The heaviest of my glass paperweights will not do it. They will not be quelled. They will not be silenced. And it is not single words alone. I speak of entire sentences, paragraphs, rustling sheets of paper. They are all jostling for pre-eminence. Each one is a story unto itself, a light to see by, a moment of revelation. Yes, that is what they are all crying out to me, all at once, during these long hours of sleeplessness.

And so to bed again. Let me lie at rest here, as I would lie flat on my tombstone, with its refreshing coolness of smooth marble in the roaring heat of high summer. It is the goodness of things that has transported me to this place, the goodness and the sheer bountifulness of all that envelops me here, in Géay, my consummate destination, my place of eternal arrival, my sweet locus of self-definition. No one can wrest me from here because I am at one with the earth beneath my feet. I soak into this earth as the drumming rain soaks into the soil. The cows browse above me. The clouds, ever changeable, keep watch over me. And she lies, my dear Marie, face down and afloat on the waters of the *Lavoir*, arms splayed, as if gently crucified. I did not carry her there. I was in no way responsible. The earth is my first and my last home. Let me lie here peaceably enough.

About the author

Michael Glover was born in Sheffield. He is currently Poetry Editor of the *Tablet* and a senior art critic and feature writer for the *Independent*. He has been a regular reviewer and commentator upon the world of poetry for the *Economist*, the *New Statesman* and the *Independent*. He has written about poetry in performance for the *Financial Times*. In 2009 he established *The Bow-Wow Shop*, a free-to-access, online poetry magazine which has been archived by the British Library.

What other poets and critics have said about Michael Glover's poetry:

'Much energy and brio' – Seamus Heaney, Nobel Prize in Literature, 1995

'Michael Glover's lines unspool gravely and efficiently with few commas – like waves that know they are on their way to someplace, but without making much fuss about it. They can be piercingly sad and hilariously wry, sometimes at the same time. Michael Glover is a major find.' – John Ashbery

'Michael Glover gives us, often dazzlingly, the poet as performer, conjuror, clown, operating with a playfulness which, whether putting forward arguments about language, reality or poetry itself, is artful and frequently highly enjoyable.' – Laurence Sail, *Stand*

'Enviably idiosyncratic and, for that reason, attractive' – Joseph Brodsky, Nobel Prize in Literature, 1987

'Michael Glover, journalist, critic and poet, writes with clarity, wit and, best of all, he makes sense of non-sense.' – Barry Fantoni, co-founder, *Private Eye*